Choices

Ruchira Khanna

Table of Contents

ACKNOWLEDGEMENT 5

ONE 6

TWO 11

THREE 19

FOUR 28

FIVE.. 37

SIX.. 47

SEVEN... 51

EIGHT 59

NINE 70

TEN 92

ELEVEN 99

TWELVE..104

THIRTEEN..108

FOURTEEN..114

FIFTEEN 121

SIXTEEN..126

SEVENTEEN...135

EIGHTEEN 150

NINETEEN 156

TWENTY 166

TWENTY ONE 172

TWENTY TWO 180

TWENTY THREE..191

TWENTY FOUR 199

TWENTY FIVE 212

Miss you, Papa!

Acknowledgement

I would like to express my gratitude to my family who stood by my choice and helped me accomplish my dream.

Thank you Ritu Lalit, my editor who helped me shape this plot.

Thank you Aditi Chopra for your tips and pointers towards publication.

One

It is nearly dawn and the October winds blow the fog across San Francisco, making visibility difficult at the correctional facility. Lights flicker in every direction discouraging any prisoner's thoughts of escape. From inside a cell, one can make out the sound of marching footsteps, melancholy tunes, and a faint light in the distance. When the light flickers, the shadows of singing guards holding flashlights dance across the darkened walls. The song keeps Mateo and his co-workers company and helps them brave the cold. They continue diligently until the first ray of sunshine breaks over their facility. They turn off their flashlights as a fresh batch of guards enters the grounds.

Their shift is over, and they retreat to their quarters. They eagerly remove their insulated jackets, gloves, and tall, pleated hats, and head to the coffee machine. Their bodies and mind yearn for repose after their long night shift. The five guards including Mateo wait in line patiently for their coffee, and then plop onto the tattered old couch, which is smeared with black marks. The couch sags beneath each man's weight, letting out a gasp of exhaustion whenever it is sat on, a desperate plea for retirement. But due to the sad state of the economy, budget cuts, and harsh economic measures, the sofa is the jailor's last priority. The guards turn on the radio. Mateo is delighted to hear that it will be a sunny day with only partial clouds. Such weather is a rare delight in San Francisco, a city plagued by damp fog and gray skies.

Mateo's wife is scheduled for a C-section today at noon, and he is looking forward to discovering whether he will have a son or daughter. He sips his coffee at the window, fervently hoping that it will be a smooth and easy operation.

Mateo's thoughts are interrupted by a buzz over the intercom. One of the guards gets up to push it. Albert, the jailer, is on the other end. He asks for Mateo to come see him before he takes his paternity leave. Mateo picks up his belongings, and his car keys, eager to head home once his meeting with Albert is done. His companions wish him luck, and the rusty old door swings shut behind him as he heads towards the Albert's office.

Mateo is a Hispanic man of average stature in his early thirties. He has a slight paunch, which he tries to keep under control with exercise and the occasional diet. He walks briskly towards the main building, as he does not want to keep the jailor waiting. His mind is filled with thoughts of his wife and baby. He reaches the door of Albert's office, which bears a burnished copper plate that reads "Albert Silva," in gold letters. Prior to knocking, he nervously adjusts his collar and shirt.

Albert's bellowing voice immediately invites him in. Albert is a tall, athletic man whose well-defined muscles bulge below the neatly rolled up sleeves of his shirt.

He signals Mateo to sit down and finishes signing off some papers. There are new cuts coming in prison, which Albert has to confirm via his signatures. Once done and papers put aside, Albert smiles and asks Mateo, "So how are you feeling? You will be a dad in a few hours."

Mateo shrugs his shoulders, and his forehead becomes sweaty, but he sounds positive and excited, "I have mixed feelings right now. I guess when I will hold the baby in my arms; I will realize my responsibilities."

Albert laughs and assures him, "You will be fine. I am sure you will do as good a job being a father as you do here, at work."

Mateo feels confident and sits up straight saying, "Thank you!" He is quick to add, "I hope I do as good a job as you have done with Leonardo."

Albert beams with delight hearing his son's name and responds, "Oh! That boy knows what he wants to do with his life. He is one determined fella." He continues, but with remorse, "Although I hope that his goal in life meets his destiny."

There is silence in the room as both the men reflect on their past and the turmoil.

Albert is quick to press the fast-forward button and comes to his present by pulling out an envelope from the drawer. He puts it in front of Mateo.

Mateo's thoughts get distracted after seeing that cover.

Confused and nervous Mateo asks, "What is it?"

Albert pushes it towards Mateo and says, "Open it"

Mateo opens it with shaky fingers because getting a pink slip right now would be really bad, pulls out a typed letter and starts to read.

Dear Mateo,

I appreciate your diligent service to this county jail, and from January 2013, I would like to give you a 5% annual hike in your salary; making it to $43,475.

Hope you keep up with your hard work and continue to make a difference in all our lives."

The letter ends with Albert's signature.

Overjoyed and overwhelmed with gratitude, Mateo stands up tearfully thanks Albert.

Albert stands up as well and clarifies, "This was supposed to be handed out in December, but I thought you needed it now to welcome a new life in your lives. You have 3 weeks of paternity leave, go ahead and bond well with your child."

Shaking Albert's hand and with his good wishes still ringing his ears, Mateo shuts the door behind him and takes a deep breath, full of happiness and relief. He walks towards his car with measured steps even though he wants to run and show the letter to his wife.

Two

Mateo looks at his watch and calculates that they have 4 hours to get to the hospital. He and his wife, Maria had been hoping for a natural birth, but their infant had refused to turn around into the proper position. Maria has been pregnant for over nine months, so the only option left is a C-section.

He takes a diversion and drives to a grocery store, grabs a bouquet of flowers and a German chocolate cake. They would celebrate his success before going to the hospital. On his way to the counter, he realizes that even though it is Maria's favorite, will not cherish this cake until the baby is born. He puts the cake back on the shelf and sees strawberries. Grabbing them along with a can of whipped cream, he smiles to himself, "This is purrrfect."

He starts to get naughty ideas and reasons that once the baby is here; there will be smelly diapers and sleepless nights, so this is just perfect. He goes to the counter to check out those items and realizes that he has left his re-usable bag in the car. So he pays for a plastic bag and rushes out.

Mateo reaches his apartment, 2 miles away from the facility. It is a one-bedroom apartment on the first floor of a gated community. He rings the bell and waits up patiently for Maria to come and open the door. He never uses his key, as he does not want to alarm her by just barging into the house.

He can hear her footsteps approaching and the lock and hides the bouquet and shopping bag behind his back.

Maria, a petite woman in her late 20's with short hair wearing maternity clothes to conceal her tummy and the extra weight she is carrying around her lower abdomen area, opens the door with a huge smile.

Mateo kisses her excitedly, forgetting his aching eyes from a sleepless night.

He is super excited about the baby-in-the-bun and the letter he is carrying in his jacket pocket. Maria kisses him back and makes way for him to enter the house. He enters with an angle with the pretext to hide the bag. Seeing the weird way of Mateo's entry, Maria asks him, "What are you hiding, honey?"

She shuts the door and turns around; Mateo surprises her with a bouquet. Maria is delighted; she takes the flowers and smells the fragrant roses while asking with curiosity, "What is the occasion, honey?"

Mateo steps into the kitchen and does not answer since; he is busy taking out the strawberries and the can of cream from the bag.

He shouts back, "Maria, please be seated. I will be right back."

Maria goes to the living room and seats herself while admiring those beautiful multi-colored roses. She calls out to Mateo, "Can you get a vase with water for these flowers?" She continues mockingly, "And before you ask me where the container is, it is under the sink."

"Sure, honey" he replies.

From the couch, she can hear the water running and dishes being taken off the shelf, and is confused. Mateo first brings out the vase, takes the flowers and removes the wrapping. He places them in the vase, making sure the flowers are arranged to her satisfaction. After placing the vase, he takes the wrapper to the kitchen. Maria smiles at him.

After a few minutes, he comes out with a bowl of strawberries and the can of cream. Maria is surprised and frowns slightly, "What are these for? I have finished eating my breakfast."

She adds anxiously, "Your breakfast is on the kitchen counter. We have to leave soon"

Mateo calms her and says, "This is a small celebration before the baby comes out. I have something to share with you."

He sits next to her, placing the strawberries and the can of cream on the side table. He reaches into the jacket pocket and pulls out the envelope, takes the letter out and gives it to Maria. She starts to read it while taking deep breaths, subconsciously preparing for her baby and the delivery. While Maria is reading the letter, he sprays some whipped cream over one strawberry and waits for her to finish reading. She is delighted on reading the letter and hugs Mateo. She is about to kiss him for his success, but he pops the strawberry with a whipped cream in her mouth, and puts the other end into his. They gaze into each other's eyes as they munch on the strawberry and finally kiss. Maria's mouth is smeared with cream, and he wipes it clean with his tongue and affection. They giggle and finish the remaining strawberries in the same way as passion peaked, but they hold back, just play with each other fondly until it is time to go.

With just an hour left, they reluctantly draw away from each other. Maria gets up to freshen herself. Mateo heats the breakfast and eats it quickly, cleans up the kitchen, and the dishes, while Maria put a bag, which needed to be taken to the hospital, near the doorway and sits down waiting to hear the words, "Let's go!"

Just then the phone rings. It's Maria's mom, who is super excited and wants to re-confirm the time of her arrival at the hospital. Mateo takes the call, confirms the time and hangs up. He glances at his wife who is anxiously fidgeting with her ring.

Sensing her anxiety, he kneels down at her feet, looks up, and whispers, "Everything is going to be fine. Do not worry. We both are in it, together."

She smiles and inhales deeply, nods, and they kiss.

Mateo takes a quick shower and changes into every day clothes. He pulls on his jeans but takes a while to decide on his shirt. He is confused on what color to wear, a blue shirt or a shirt with pink stripes. He places both the shirts on the bed and shut his eyes, turns around and picks a shirt with eyes still shut and quickly wears it. He opens his eyes and sees that he is wearing a blue colored shirt, gets excited, quickly slaps on after-shave, he goes into the living room and declares joyously that they will have a baby boy.

Maria, who is putting away the salary hike letter of Mateo in a file cabinet, turns around, and smiles and while putting her hand on her belly, she whispers, "Daddy has come to know our little secret."

Mateo is surprised at this comment. Maria smiles and explains, "I had this notion that it is a boy since the second trimester, but did not share the news with you since you wanted it to be a surprise."

Mateo grins and hugs her. They both check their paperwork and insurance cards and started heading out. Maria pauses a little as if in double mind, and then announces that she ought to use the bathroom. Mateo nods. Once done, she opens the drawer next to the basin and pulls out her cross pendant, a simple silver cross with a white gold chain. Before her pregnancy, she wore her pendant around her neck. Towards the second trimester, her swelling made it uncomfortable to wear. Holding the string, she kisses the cross and takes it with her and goes out. Mateo locks their apartment after her, and they walk towards the car. He puts the bag in his trunk where a toddler car seat was sitting all wrapped up in a box, and smiles recalling the fun they had when his colleagues at work gave them an amazing surprise baby shower. One of his colleague's wives had invited Maria to the workplace for a surprise luncheon. Maria agreed after a lot of coaxing. When she entered a loud voice said, "Surprise" Maria was taken aback. She turned around to see that all of Mateo's colleagues and some wives had gathered to give them a baby shower.

Albert and his wife, Amelia had arranged this baby shower for the couple. With everyone's contribution, they managed to get a car seat, 3 months supply of diapers, and a stroller. This is the best gift for the to-be parents and they got all emotional while receiving the shower gifts. Mateo's colleagues in the county jail are his second family.

Mateo has been a guard at this correctional facility for 4 years and is glad that he listened to his dad and gave up working as a mechanic, even though it was his passion. This job had given him stability to marry his high school sweetheart, Maria.

Once at the hospital, they nervously walk to the maternity ward. An elderly woman with a nametag, "Sylvia" is behind the front desk. She greets the first time parents with a smile and hands them a couple of papers, which they fill in and hand them back.

Once the formalities are done, Mateo and Maria observe all the baby pictures around them on the wall. They are fascinated by each one of them while pointing and whispering to each other.

Just then Sylvia tells them, "Your room is ready." They follow Sylvia into the room. She is a pleasant woman who has seen many deliveries in this hospital. Sensing their nervousness, she assures Maria that she would be fine, gets her changed into the hospital gown and leaves, after informing them that the nurse will soon come to check her stats.

After some time, the nurse Lucy enters, meets Maria and strikes up a small conversation with Maria while she inserts a needle for an intravenous line (IV), which will be used during the procedure. Fetal monitor is put to watch the status of the baby. This is essential to monitor the safety of the mom-to-be and the baby. Patches are also applied to the chest, arms and legs to get an electrocardiogram (EKG), which will help record the electrical activity of her heart during the C-section. After wiring up Maria, she wishes her best of luck and says that the doctor will come by shortly.

Mateo and Maria look at each other and smile as they squeeze each other's hands and get ready for whatever destiny has to offer.

Dr. Shukla, Maria's gynecologist knocks the door and Mateo get up to greet her. She comes in and wishes Maria, checks the records of the patient and the EKG. She asks the couple if they have any questions for her. Mateo who is getting very nervous looking at all the stuff attached to Maria asks, "Doctor, I hope all this wiring around my wife is safe for her and the baby."

The doctor smiles and assures him, "Mr. Lopez, as of now things look normal. I am sure that the delivery will go smoothly, unless things change."

She left the room giving the couple a few minutes to themselves before Maria is taken into the operating room. Just then, they hear a knock on the door, and before Mateo could go and answer it, Maria's parents and Mateo's dad throw the door open and enter, speaking in Hispanic. Mateo gets up and hugs them. Maria extends her arm towards her mom, Isabelle. She has always been her rock and inspiration, and was glad to see her during this hour.

Three

Maria's mom, Isabelle had led a hard life. At a young age of 18, she lost her parents in a natural disaster. Everything around her was in shambles, and she had nowhere to go. But, being a strong woman she overcame many hurdles and immigrated to the United States, and then came to San Ramon, California where her friend, Leila had been living for 2 years, and was working for a professional cleaning company.

Leila resigned from the company and along with Isabella, started a cleaning company by the name of 'L&I Cleaning Services'. They would drive to different addresses and clean homes and offices. Leila already had experience and also had quite a few customers who knew her and liked her work, and that gave their company an initial boost. Isabella was a quick learner. Both were zealous and diligent.

Isabelle and Leila used to take Mondays off from cleaning. That was the day they would clean their apartment and finish off with their chores such as laundry, cleaning, grocery etc. That was also the day they used to dress up and visit clubs. On Mondays, they visited their favorite bar, which was downtown and offered a happy hour from 5pm to 7pm. Their weekly visits made them the regulars there, and the manager and the waitresses knew them. They had to just say, "The usual" when ordering their drinks.

Two men who were in their late 20's were regulars there too. They used to work in an Auto Spa two blocks away, where automobiles were cleaned and pampered by the best of accessories. Isabelle and Leila started eyeing these two Hispanic men who were medium built, always wore a smile and could speak English. The men noticed their interest and introduced themselves as Javier and Adrian.

Javier was in late 20's and had a whitish complexion. He had a habit of fidgeting with his hands when speaking. Aware of this habit he would consciously hold his key chain in one hand so that his hands did not go places when he approached Isabelle. Adrian got friendly with Leila.

Soon their friendship turned into serious relationships. Since they were all immigrants and had no families here, they decided to get married on the same day, went for a weeklong honeymoon to different locations and returned to work.

Leila moved with Adrian into his apartment, which fortunately was just over a mile away from Isabelle and Javier's home. Life was smooth. Silicon Valley was booming with Tech jobs, and that came, long hours at work. L&I Cleaning Company flourished since people did not have time to clean their homes. Adrian and Javier continued working together at the Car Spa.

Both the families were able to create their own world by changing their perception, and putting their knowledge into practice.

Isabelle conceived Maria in a year's time.

Leila had difficulty getting pregnant, and finally after five years of their marriage, they welcomed a baby girl into their home. They named her Chelsea. Maria was like an older sister to Chelsea, and they went to the same school. Once Maria outgrew her clothes, they went to Chelsea who wore them happily as she loved Maria's style.

Maria met Mateo in High School when she was pursuing English literature. Their relationship withstood a lot of storms. She was his strength when he lost his mom to prolonged illness. Mateo and Maria parted for a few years when Maria went to San Diego State University to pursue her under graduation, and Mateo went to a community college to pursue his dream of becoming a car mechanic.

Mateo and his dad, Eron became frequent visitors to Isabelle and Javier's house for meals and emotional comfort. Mateo and Maria were in touch even though their college education kept them apart for four years. Their relationship matured with each passing year, and their love for each other grew stronger. Mateo intended to give a name to their relationship once he had a steady job. Alas, his hopping from one garage to another in search of a full time gig as a car mechanic was not rendering much success. Maria was getting impatient with this.

After a few years of hopping from one garage to another, Mateo finally listened to his dad to look into becoming a guard for a correctional facility. He enrolled in a yearlong training. Meanwhile, Maria finished her graduation and moved back to her parent's home. She started looking for a job and managed to find a job as a librarian in her county library.

After rigorous training at a corrections academy, Mateo got his certification and became a state guard. It was a big ceremony, and Mateo invited Maria and her family to attend this significant event along with his dad, Eron. When Mateo got on the stage to get his certificate, he kept touching his pocket to check for a status of something that was bulging. That was a distraction to Maria, and she was confused about his constant fidgeting. After the event, he took Maria out for a dinner date and fished out a jewel box from his bulging pocket. She was happy and emotional. She allowed him to put that ring on her finger and admired it with teary eyes. She kissed the ring and Mateo.

Mateo's intention of defining his relationship with Maria was the magic, which orchestrated infinity of details and his action activated the line of events.

Mateo got a guard job in a correctional facility in San Francisco, (SF). Within a few months, they got married and moved to SF city. Maria got a transfer from her existing job in a local library near her new home.

They were a happy couple and shared their adventures and laughter when they would meet up after their long 8 hours at work. There were times when Maria would see Mateo after two days if Mateo had his night shift and would return the next morning. This couple had weathered so many storms together that it did not matter to them. Their love was strong and just speaking to each other made their day.

****

Now four years later, Maria is lying on the hospital bed with the intravenous line (IV) and the EKG monitor and is all set to be transported into the operating room for her C-Section. When Isabelle sees her in this state, her strong heart melts and she hugs her child fondly. Maria gives her mom the silver cross and asks her to hold onto it until she comes out. Isabelle nods and kisses it.

There is a knock on the door. Sylvia and Lucy come in with another male helper who introduces himself as Gil. They drag the bed on wheels into the operating room. Mateo is given a costume to wear so that he can join in the operating room to cut the umbilical cord. Dr. Shukla greets Maria and Mateo's parents who are anxiously standing outside; as she walks in the operating room.

Approximately after thirty minutes, a nurse comes out of the operating room to inform the couple's parents that they have been blessed with a boy and congratulate them. The grandparents are ecstatic and start thanking the Lord for all that they have received till date.

After a few hours, Maria is wheeled back to her room. Mateo is beside her. Her parents and father-in-law congratulate them.

After an hour or so, baby Lopez arrives in the room. He weighs 7 pounds and 8 ounces, is 11 inches tall and excels in his Apgar score. Parents and Grandparents drool over his crib and compare his features with his parents. Mateo whispers to Maria and goes out of the room and sits down on a bench.

Breathing a big sigh of relief, he pulls out his late mom's picture, speaks a few words to her and puts the picture back in his pocket. He then calls his boss, Albert and announces the birth of his baby boy. He is so excited that he goes on about his weight, his Apgar score and how he looks. Albert lets him speak. When the proud dad pauses, Albert says, "Congratulations, Mateo. I hope Maria is fine."

Mateo blushes since he has just talked about the baby and not mentioned his wife even once. He says, "Oh yes, I am sorry. She is fine and as happy as me. We both are blessed to have a baby."

Albert inquires about visiting hours and says that he and his wife will visit them the next day. Mateo says, "Please tell the others at the facility." Albert says, "Sure, I will Mateo. See you tomorrow."

Mateo hangs up and then goes through his contact list to inform other friends about the good news. This time, he makes sure to mention Maria before someone asks about her. After making all the calls, he returns to the room where his dad and his in-laws are still drooling away on this bundle of joy. There is laughter everywhere, and he is filled with gratitude to see everyone happy. It is such a rare visitor in their household.

Sylvia comes in to inform that the visitation hours are over, and mother and baby need to rest. Grand parents get up as if forced to and promise to return the next day. Isabelle has brought Mateo dinner and reminds him to heat and eat it as she leaves.

Dr. Shukla drops in, checks on Maria, and satisfied that the patient is doing fine, goes, telling her to rest well and ask for help if and when needed.

Baby Lopez's pediatrician, Dr. Halpin comes, checks on the baby, reassures the parents and advises them on keeping the baby in the nursery so that Maria can rest. So, Baby Lopez is kept in the nursery for the night. While having dinner, the new parents start thinking of a name for the baby and settle on Pedro, which means "as a rock" It's a good name, a sound name for their son, who will be as strong as a rock when any difficulty strikes in his life and not melt down. After their dinner, the night nurse, Katie comes, introduces herself and bids them a good night.

Mateo turns the sofa into a sleeping bed, lies down, and says, "Honey, I am glad things turned out fine. I am pretty sure our future is bright with our boy."

Maria is too tired to have this discussion she mumbles, "Hmm" and dozes off. Mateo turns on his side and hopes that his son gets to meet his wish and destiny at the same junction. For some reason, he recalls his own dream of becoming a car mechanic even though his destiny has made him work as a Guard of a correctional facility. A strong wave of yearning for his passion engulfs him, but he suppresses it. He cannot tell Maria and besides, with a kid, he needs to be there to support his family.

Mateo made a decision to control his own choices, thus controlling his fate at this junction.

Next morning, nurse Katie arrives, checks on her patient, helps her freshen up and change. Breakfast arrives, and Maria realizes how ravenous she is. While she is eating, Mateo goes to the cafeteria for his own breakfast.

Nurse Katie arrives with the baby and guides Maria on how to start nursing her infant and how the baby will clutch on to her breast. She is still bonding with the baby when Mateo arrives with his cup of Joe and a sandwich. He is delighted to see this and kisses Maria on her forehead. Maria is in tears.

The baby is whisked away before the visiting hours to seclude the baby from visitors.

Four

The first visit is from the county registrar. He wants to know if the Lopez parents have decided on a name. The parents nod, and he gives them a form to fill up, and tells them to leave the completed form at the front desk; with Nurse Sylvia, and tells them that the birth certificate will be mailed to their home address.

Mateo fills out the form carefully and feels proud to write his son's name for the first time, "Pedro Lopez". He shows the form to Maria and she checks for any errors. She nods with a gentle smile. Mateo takes the form and drops it off at the nurse's station. Sylvia checks the form and says, "Nice name."

Mateo smiles and says, "Thank you."

Maria's parents arrive with all sorts of goodies in their bags. They bring breakfast and lunch for Mateo, balloons and a bouquet of flowers, and sweets. Mateo, awed at seeing all of this says, "Guys, you did not have to do so much." Isabelle hugs him and says, "Shh, keep quiet" Maria smiles and extends her arm to hug her mom and dad.

Eron enters after a while with a bag full of baby clothes. He gives it to Mateo and said, "I tried to shop the best I could. Here is the receipt just in case, you want to exchange them."

Mateo hugs his dad and said, "They will be perfect, dad."

Eron has a teary smile.

Maria sees all this from her bed, and waves at Eron and said, "Thank you so much for all that you are doing." Eron came towards her, and hugs her.

There is a knock on the door and Mateo goes to open it. It is Albert and his wife, Amelia. They have a bouquet of flowers in their hand. Mateo shakes hands with his boss, he steps aside, and gestured them to come in. Albert and Amelia congratulate Maria. Mateo introduces his dad and his in-laws to them. They greet each other. Then there is an uncomfortable pause. Isabelle, quick to sense it, brings out the sweets. She offers to all and again, the conversation starts flowing. Albert asks about the baby. Mateo announces, "We have named our baby, Pedro." The grandparents are thrilled and start hugging the parents. Albert and Amelia wait for their turn to congratulate them.

Mateo inquires about their son, Leonardo. Albert replies with pride, "Leonardo is doing fine. He is currently a sophomore in High School and eyeing on some pre-requisites from the community college for his undergraduate degree. He plans to pursue a bachelor's degree in Computer Science." Mateo is happy to learn about Leonardo's progress. He has seen Leonardo grow into a fine teenager and has always exchanged pleasantries with him whenever he visited his dad's office. He asks Mateo to wish him luck on his behalf, and the proud father smiles and nods.

The jailor and his wife get up and bid their byes to them. Mateo goes out to see them off. The warden shakes hands with him and wishes him luck.

Warden and Amelia start walking out of the hospital to their car. Amelia is a short, slim lady in her late 30's and is beautiful inside and out. She is a very strong willed person and is the pillar of strength to her then toddler son and husband when they were forced to leave Portugal and emigrate to the United States of America. Her small income was the only source of livelihood for her family.

Now Leonardo is 15-years-old, as tall as his dad and has a few freckles on his cheek. He is highly ambitious, and is aware that he lives in a land of opportunity. He has never been pressurized by his parents, but has always had high aspirations. Albert is just happy that Leonardo is on the right track but Amelia worries and hopes that Leonardo's dreams come true or else he would also be bitter and shattered like his dad. She did not have the courage at this point to be of emotional support to another individual in their household.

Leonardo is in tenth grade, but is always in a hurry to submit his projects, and feels if he is on top of academics, he can briskly move to the next grade. He excels academically despite the pressure he puts on himself. Steve Jobs awes him and his autobiography is Leonardo's bible. Amelia is always lecturing him to slow down but Albert defends him, so Leonardo does not change.

He plays basketball and is in his school's team. His tall build makes it easier for him to score well and makes him popular with his teammates. Leonardo is humble and always says that it is teamwork that makes them the winning team, he is grounded even though he is popular.

He is popular with the girls in school because of his credits. But he has no time for anybody. He is focused on his goals, his future and his projects.

Just like his mother, his teachers, even though they at first admired his momentum, soon advised him to slow down. But Leonardo was a man on a mission. It was like he had boarded a train to reach a destination, if the train was slow or made many stops, he would try to hop into another train going in that direction.

In his junior year, Leonardo had already started applying for colleges around California so that he could get an idea of the course work and also the courses he could do at a community college, and get them transferred to his desired University. He is aware how cost effective this method of studying would be thus, wanted to pursue that route.

On the first day of his senior year, he meets with an accident. A motorist hits him, while he was crossing the street to enter his school. He is injured badly and has to be admitted to the hospital. His parent's rush to the hospital and see, to their surprise, many students flocked around his room. Fearing the worst, they pushed through them to see their son.

Leonardo is lying in bed with his left leg and right arm in plaster, smiling at students signing on his plaster. A relieved Albert goes up to his son and puts his hand over his head, "How are you feeling, Leonardo?"

Leonardo says, "I am okay dad, just bummed up that this was my first day as a senior in school and I will be lying here until my plaster is removed."

Amelia caresses his forehead and says, "Everything will be alright. You can still study while bandaged. Your friends can get your assignments."

Leonardo frowns at the mention of friends. He never made one. He was too busy running on a mission. The high schoolers who were signing his bandages all agreed with Leonardo's mom and said, "Sure"

Leonardo is overwhelmed and says, "Thank you." He is ashamed to ask them their names. He had never really cared to be friends with anybody but they were here for him. He is embarrassed, but also filled with gratitude. An attractive girl standing in one corner of the room can't stop looking at him. Albert notices this, and likes the way she was admiring Leonardo. Since Leonardo is being awkward, he announces loudly, "You all have been so nice to my son that I want to just capture this moment. If you all may, please allow me to take a picture of you all around him, it will be great."

The high schoolers smile and gather around the bed. Amelia gets up and goes out of the room to give them space. Albert clicks many pictures from different angles.

Amelia goes to the nurse's station to inquire about the status of her son. The nurse pages the doctor. Dr. Henry comes by in a few minutes to the station. He is a tall middle-aged man with a few wrinkles on his face, possibly because of stress and the environment he is working in. Amelia shakes hands with the doctor introducing herself as Leonardo's mother, "How is my son doing? Anything serious?"

Dr. Henry guides her gently to the couch and after they both sit down, he explains, " Leonardo has suffered some blows to his ligaments of the left leg and right arm. We also see a hairline fracture. It will take approximately 3-4 weeks to recover, which includes his physical therapy."

Amelia asks, "So, when can he go home?"

Dr. Henry said, "Let's keep him for 24 hours. He can go home after that."

Amelia, thanks the doctor, gets up and goes to the room. The teenagers are now leaving after shaking hands with Albert who has a word or two for everybody as they leave, especially the girl who was eyeing Leonardo.
Amelia enters the now empty room, sits near Leonardo and tells him what the doctor said. Leonardo gets frustrated and turns his head away from her. She can understand his frustration and

tries to console him by patting his shoulder, "Things happen for a reason. Look at the plus side of this incident; you realize that you have friends. Earlier, you were so busy with deadlines and your own issues that you never paused to see who all were with you. Reflect on it and be gracious to the students who bring you your assignments."

Leonardo turns to face her and nods, "You are right, mom. I sure did learn a lot today. I have always been on the run and have never helped anyone. Today so many of them came to see me. I am grateful to them" She kisses his forehead with tenderness and pride.

Albert hears the whole conversation, and wants to lighten the mood so he starts showing the pictures that he clicked via his phone to Leonardo. Albert picks the right moment to point the girl to Leonardo. When Leonardo was zooming in on the group picture, he points the girl to him, asking him if he knows her. Leonardo hesitates a bit then shrugs his shoulder, "Oh yeah, she is my junior, uh maybe."

Albert and Amelia are kind of happy to hear that response, and exchange glances, smiling with relief that their son also has those kinds of feelings. Albert winks at Amelia. Albert starts pulling Leonardo's leg, "Hmm interesting. I wonder what she was doing here since she is your junior. Any idea, Leonardo?" Leonardo blushes, "I have no idea, Dad. Maybe she was carpooling with someone so had to come along."

"Sure, maybe" admitted Albert still looking at the picture. "But, I like this girl, she is sweet and I liked how she was glancing at you from the corner of a room." Leonardo is embarrassed and brushes his dad's shoulder with his right hand. They all laugh.

Amelia says, "Albert, could you arrange something for us to eat since we are going to have to spend the night in the hospital."

Albert replies, "Leonardo I am thinking of getting Chinese food. So, would you like to join us for dinner or would you like to eat the hospital food?" Leonardo winked back at him and says, "Dad, you kidding, right? I would rather eat the Chinese food. Get it, dad."

They high-five, Albert winks at his wife and goes to get the food for his family.

There is a knock on the door and Amelia gets up to let the nurse, Mary, in. She has come in to check on Leonardo and show him the menu for the dinner. Leonardo is not interested in the hospital menu and he refuses politely. Mary is confused and says, "Leonardo, you need to take your medicines so, food is essential."

Amelia smiles and tells her, "His dad is getting Chinese for him." Nurse Mary smiles; "I understand" She goes out and fetches a small tray, which had his medicines in it. She explains the dosage to Amelia who takes note.

Mary asks, "So, which of the parent will be staying the night here? We can accommodate only one parent, unfortunately." Amelia says, "Oh sure, not a problem. His dad will have dinner with us and leave for the night. I will be staying back with my son. It is just one night stay, so we should be fine." The nurse smiles, and gets some sheets for her. She asks Amelia to page them if there are any issues during the night and leaves.

Leonardo has his headphones over his ears and is listening to his favorite music when his dad arrives with the food. Amelia serves them while Albert turns on the television. Leonardo is told to remove his headphones, and he obeys. The Silva family has a family dinner sharing a laugh or two over some random television show. The accident was unfortunate but with good food and in each other's company, they share a happy evening.

After dinner, disposable dishes are trashed, and Albert stays with them until Leonardo has his medicines, and kisses his son and wife good night, promises to come by early morning next day, and leaves.

Albert makes a detour to the correctional facility to see how things are. He had left abruptly in the middle of the day and there were unresolved issues that needed attention. Parking his car at his usual spot, he walks to his office, while paging Peter, a registered nurse working at this facility. He frowns when the call is not answered, as Peter has always been very efficient and prompt, his pager is always by his side.

Five

Albert unlocks his office, turns on the light and sees an envelope on the floor, which must have been pushed from under his door. He picks it up and heads to his desk. It is sealed so he has to use a letter opener to slide under its flap and open it. He sits down while opening the letter and starts to read. While reading, his forehead's knits up and he rubs it with his finger. He throws the paper on the desk and dials Dr. Beringer's number, and asks him to come to see him in a stern voice. He put down the phone and folds both his hands under his chin and keeps staring at the letter lying on his desk.

There is a knock on the door, Dr. Beringer enters, he is about 5 feet 3 inches, with a medium build is bald, wears a pair of glasses, and is dressed in a white lab coat over his guard uniform. Albert gets up and asks him to be seated.

"So, what is this all about?" asks Albert pushing the letter towards the physician.

The doctor glances at the letter and says, "Peter was quite unhappy with the situation which he felt was life threatening. I tried to make him understand that it is just one prisoner and we will deal with it, but he did not listen and wrote this resignation and dropped it off at your office."

Albert says, "I need the history of the prisoner. I want to get into the bottom of this."

He very humbly requests, "Sir, it will be good if we allow Peter to go. The patient, Ricardo is not an easy convict. He has many connections and we all will get into deep trouble if we dig deeper into his profile."

Albert is furious and comes to his feet shouting, "What nonsense! We are running a correctional facility and if we don't try to correct a behavior of a convict, it will be shameful for us, and also for the reputation of this place. Get me the details on what really happened and how it went out of hand compelling Peter to resign. I need information, Robert."

Robert agrees to get the details by tomorrow noon. Albert thanks him and shakes his hand as he departs. Outside the office, Robert grumbles, "Stupid jailor, he will land us all into trouble."

Dr. Robert Beringer is born in the United States. His parents emigrated from Italy due to the fear of many mafia gangs. Till date, Robert and his parents have not visited their home in Italy. He is aware of the power these gangs wield and how they can crush a common man.

Albert takes care of some more pending paperwork, signs some papers that need his attention and calls the night shift guard. Once he is satisfied that things are fine, he prepares a memo on Peter's resignation since he is sure that in the morning this news will spread like wildfire, and he wants everything in control.

He locks his office goes to his car, his mind on Peter and his own family that he has to pick up the next day from the hospital. All of a sudden things seem crazy, but he knew they would be smooth sailing in some time.

He wakes up early the next day since he wants to swing by his office before he picks up his family, packs fresh clothes for both of them and puts them in the trunk of his car. Reaches the facility where things looked a little tense due to Peter's abrupt resignation. Albert unlocks his office, pages his secretary and asks her to send the memo to each department.

It is a memo to all the heads of department calling them for a meeting. He is certain that by late afternoon, his family will be home and Dr. Beringer would have given him the detailed background of Peter's resignation.

Once this is done, he leaves for the hospital. At the hospital he first stops by at the nurse's station to inquire about Leonardo and the checkout procedure. He enters the room and is delighted to meet his family. Amelia hugs and kisses him and he responds, it is a love that has matured over the years especially with the hardships they faced.

Albert comes to his son's bed and asks, "How was your night in this Sanitarium, buddy?" Leonardo chuckles and executes a high five with his dad, "I am much better today. The pain is under control and if the doc approves, I can even go to school. My friends will help me out," He winks at his parents. Amelia did not find it funny and said, "No way, Junior Silva. You are not going to school until you are bandage free." Albert chuckles and says, "Lighten up, honey."

Dr. Henry and his nurse knock prior to entering. Albert signs the required paperwork for the wheelchair Leonardo will use until his plaster is removed. The nurse says, "The person who bumped his car into Leonardo will be paying a lump sum for his treatment so you can expect credit in your account." Albert nods and signs as the doctor examines Leonardo and say he can be discharged.

After last minute instructions and the prescriptions, he shakes hands with Leonardo's parents, and wishes the boy a speedy recovery.

Once ready, Albert helps his son into the wheelchair and wheels him to the car, followed by Amelia. Even though Albert's mind is at the facility, he smiles and asks his family if they would like to make a stop anywhere for breakfast. Leonardo, who was about to put his earplugs to listen to music; he interrupts his action and says, "Sure, dad. Thanks."

Amelia looks at Albert with an appreciative smile, as she knows her husband is very particular about being at work on time and did not like to miss his duties.

They stop at iHop and Amelia gets down, takes the chair from the trunk, and Albert helps Leonardo get into it. Being a weekday morning, there is no waiting and they are escorted to their table immediately.

Albert orders his usual, country fried steak and eggs. Amelia asks for her Simple and fit two-egg breakfast. Leonardo is debating between a smokehouse combo and his dad's selection. Albert senses the confusion, "Why don't we share, Leonardo? I would love to have a bite from your smokehouse combo."

A jar of orange juice is ordered along with 2 cups of coffee.

Albert pulls out his phone and starts checking for messages while waiting for their orders. The message he is expecting has not arrived so he diverts his attention by seeing the pictures that he clicked yesterday of his son and his friends and that special girl. He shows one such group picture that had the girl in the forefront to Leonardo, who is sitting across him. "So, your friends, will be swinging by our home quite often now, huh? I am guessing this special girl will also come by to check on you."

Leonardo checks the picture, and sees the girl with an innocent smile striking an elegant pose. "Hmm, sure my friends will come and update me on my assignments. This is one thing I don't want to trail behind especially with my final year at school. And if Sophia wants to come by, she is more than welcome."

He utters her name unknowingly in a very natural way. Amelia and Albert look at each other, smile and repeat, "Sophia"

Leonardo gets conscious and looks down, "Oh yeah, didn't I tell you that she is a year junior to me?"

"Oh sure, you did, Leonardo but you were uncertain of her name." Amelia joked.

They all have a good laugh. The waitress comes with the food; and asks Leonardo, "Oh what happened to you, poor boy!"

Leonardo just waves his other hand, and she is tactfully placing the food on the table says, "Enjoy"

The three of them start to dig in ravenously and enjoy their breakfast thoroughly. Dad and son share their combo meals and wipe the plates clean.

The waitress gets the bill and says, "Have a nice day and you young man get rid of those bandages soon." She winks at him and smiles.

Leonardo pushes his hair back and smiles back, "Sure, I will. Thanks."

Albert helps him back into the car while Amelia folds the wheelchair and keeps it in the trunk.

Albert starts the car and drives them home, parking it in the driveway, since he has to leave for work. When he's helping Leonardo out of the car, the boy asks, "Dad did you get any mail addressed to me last evening?"

"Sure, son your mail is in your room." Amelia pushes the wheelchair as Albert unlocks the front door.

They enter the living room, adjacent to the kitchen. Located past the living room are two bedrooms adjacent to each other with attached bathrooms. However, Leonardo's bathroom has two doors, one from his bedroom and the other from the living room.

Albert steps into the kitchen for a bottle of water and waits patiently for his wife who is busy settling their son in his room. Once she comes out of Leonardo's room, they hug each other, grateful that things worked out fine. Amelia says, "This incident will help him pause a bit and get new friends. It could be a way to get him closer to that pretty girl, Slyia."

Albert corrects her, "No, it is Sophia"

Both laugh.

Albert holds her close and says, "Some issues have arisen at work which made Peter resign abruptly."

Amelia has a scared look on her face as if wanting to know more. Albert says, "I have no clue what's happening. Dr. Beringer will come up with the investigation soon. I have scheduled a meeting in the evening with all the department heads, so I might be quite late tonight."

Amelia closes her eyes and brings her forehead close to Albert's, and he bends down to meet her forehead with his. She murmurs softly, "I am sure you will nail this problem down. May the Almighty guide you to make the right decision. Good luck, honey."

Albert is amused over her words and replies, "I got to solve it. I cannot flee to another country this time."
Amelia is taken aback by his response. She wants to argue with him over this comment, but gets interrupted by his kiss.

Albert goes in to check on Leonardo, who is sitting on the bed and opening up the letters he has received. Leonardo wanted to pursue a bachelor's degree in Computer Science and the envelopes have stamps from California State University Fullerton (CSUF), Fresno State, San Francisco State University (SFSU), and California State University of San Marcos (CSUSM). He has received letters and applications from all over the state. He is aiming for State Universities since they are cheaper and offer federal grants and he does not want to burden his dad financially. He is writing down all the important dates in his special notebook, so that he can fill out the necessary applications and send them in time. He is also eyeing on the courses that he could take up from the community college so that he can save on the lodging and fees and eventually get them transferred to his selected university. He is so engrossed in this that he does not see his dad standing at the doorstep.

Albert clears his throat deliberately and Leonardo looks up, "Hey dad, sorry I did not see you come in."

Albert enters and hugs his son and kisses him on his head, "I am heading to work and will be late. Take your medicines on time so that you heal fast, go to school and meet Sophia."

Leonardo grins, "Dad! Stop teasing me."

"No, son it is normal to have crushes at this age. I would give you a green signal if you were waiting up for my approval."

Leonardo laughs, "Sure, thanks dad. I would like to know Sophia since those pictures sure indicate that she is interested in me. I was always skeptical about it and so I did not have the courage to start such a conversation with her. Those pictures sure helped me, dad."
Albert proclaims, "It sure did son. After all I am your father. I knew you would need a push to start."

Leonardo's mouth falls open and he protests, "A push, seriously Dad? Am I so duh?"

"No, not at all. You are not duh, my son, but you are an introvert. Besides you are a very responsible teenager focused on your main goal in life. Your mom and I always feared that you would not enjoy other aspects of being a teenager. We have always encouraged you to go to parties, make friends and enjoy your teens. I am happy that you are looking into all that now."

Leonardo smiles with understanding and says, "Thanks, Dad."

After hugging him, Albert goes to his room and wears his uniform. When all dressed up, he pops into the kitchen where Amelia was cooking lunch and has already fixed his sandwich and put it in a brown bag. He picks it up and tells her to take it easy. He adds, with a chuckle, "And make sure you are all fresh to hear my side of the story when I return."

Amelia assures him with a hand on his shoulder," Honey, I will be all ears for your story and I wish you good luck. Stay focused and do not let anger make you take any harsh decisions."

Six

Amelia is aware of her husband's past and how he fights to keep his temper under control. He made many enemies in the past because he reacted with anger without listening to their side of the story. Gradually and with conscious effort he learnt to watch for the trigger signs, and also check such lapses before opening his mouth or making a decision. He had come to peace with his wishes in life versus what destiny had offered him. He found peace when his ex-inmates turned out to be good citizens and lived a good life.

Amelia played a major role in his change so he relies on her and always wants to know her decision before plunging into anything serious or making his own decisions.

Amelia locks the door behind Albert and informs Leonardo while placing the phone next to him, "I am going for a shower."

Leonardo keeps the phone near him and nods. He is still working on his paperwork for different schools. He is a very methodical person, just like his dad and is making the right columns to enter information for each school so that all relevant information will be available to him at a glance.

Amelia takes a leisure bath while her thoughts are with her husband. She says a silent prayer for him asking the spirits to guide him and protect him during this challenging time.

She is interrupted in her thoughts by a telephone ring and pins her ear to the door hoping that Leonardo answers it. The phone stops ringing and she hears Leonardo say, "Hello" She quickly wears her daily attire of jeans and semi formal shirts and rushes out in case the call is from Albert and he needs to speak to her.

She approaches Leonardo's room and stops as soon as she realizes the call is for Leonardo. She takes a U-turn and goes to her room to finish dressing up. Amelia is a woman of simple tastes but she loves her trinkets and her soft floral perfumes that she sprays upon her petite frame.

She steps out of her room and can hear him deep in conversation. She starts cleaning up the living room and waits up patiently for her son to hang up the phone so that she can get an update on who the caller was.

Finally after ten minutes, she hears Leonardo say, "Bye". She found those ten minutes really long, however; and enters his room with the pretext of taking his dirty clothes for laundry. While she is picking up his hamper, she asks casually, "So, who was on the phone, honey?"

Leonardo who is about to put on his headphone over his ears pauses to reply, "It was one of my friends from high school. His name is Darren and he will be coming by drop off some papers from my class, and also the assignments which are due by next week."

Amelia likes how things are evolving for her son. Finally, he has someone visiting him regarding schoolwork just like normal teens. She chirps enthusiastically, "Okey dokey"

Amelia starts the washer, cleans up her living area and soon its noon. She shouts out from the kitchen, "Leonardo would you like your supper, now?" Leonardo replies, "Sure mom thanks."

Amelia has made an Avocado sandwich with tomato soup. She places two dishes on a tray with two cups of soup and brings it in her son's room. Leonardo is delighted to see two plates, which means mom is joining him for lunch. He keeps his music and headphone aside, gets help to go on his wheelchair to go to the restroom to wash up prior to eating. They have a pleasant meal together, along with good conversation and laughter. After giving him his afternoon medication Amelia asks him to take a nap. He smiles and obeys with a wink. Amelia tries to pull his nose and he turns his face away to avoid it.

After tucking Leonardo in, she kisses his forehead and murmurs, "Leonardo, this so reminds me of the days when you were a toddler. I love going back in time, my son." She picks up the cordless phone from his room and goes to the kitchen while he smiles and closes his eyes.
Amelia cleans up the kitchen and the dishes, plans

the menu for dinner and goes in her room to lie down for a bit. She is tempted to ring up her husband, but refrains, as she knows that he would be in a meeting and does not want to disturb him. She just sends him good vibes.

She dials her friend Amy and informs her about Leonardo's accident and excuses herself from their knitting meets until her teen is back to school. Amy is her knitting buddy and carpool friend. They both were members of a knitting club, which met every Thursday at the local library. They would knit small items and donate them to shelters around the neighborhood.

Amy is sorry to hear about the accident and wishes Leonardo speedy recovery, and tells Amelia to call her anytime she needs help. Amelia is touched by her friend's gesture and thanks her and hangs up. She lies on her bed and it feels so good, as though she was away from it for a long time. So much has happened since she last lay on it. While she ponders over it, she drifts off to sleep.

Seven

Albert reaches work and feels the tension around him subside a bit. He is dealing with some paperwork left for him on his table by his secretary and waiting patiently for the clock to strike 12pm.

Mateo knocks his door and Albert happily greets him, "Hi Mateo, how have you been? I heard you had resumed work. So tell me how are your son and Maria doing?"

Mateo is pleased that his boss remembers his family. It is usually tough for a boss who heads about 4,000 employees to remember names and make the connections.

Mateo replies, "We all are doing fine. My son Pedro is two years old. He is my stress buster and my wife has joined back work."

Albert listened attentively and asks, "So, where do you keep the baby when the mom goes to work?"

"Pedro is under the care of my mother-in-law. Our parents were not happy when we booked our son a spot in a day care. They did not want their grandson going to one and insisted that they look after him. So, until he starts school, my wife's parents have taken over the responsibility to look after him." Albert was amazed by the love, "Wow, that's wonderful, Mateo. I am so happy for you guys."

Mateo thanks him and pulls out some pictures of Pedro, "I wanted to show you some of my son's latest pictures."

Albert moves closer to take a look at them, "Wow, he is adorable. My wife would also be very happy to know his progress when I tell her."

Mateo sits for a while with Albert and tries to find out more about Peter's resignation, but his boss is too professional to give him any details. He just says firmly, "Mateo, I will have a meeting with your head in the evening after I have all the details. I am sure he will update you all."
Mateo can sense the irritation in his boss' tone so he ends the topic and looks around the room as if to cool down the atmosphere, gets up, shakes hands with his boss and leaves. Albert looks at his watch, takes a sip of water and goes back to work.

Paperwork concerning each convict comes to him. With so many programs being run at the facility for the betterment of these criminals, a daily log is kept on their improvement and response to these programs. Albert always takes keen interest in them, individually.

His aim is that once the culprit leaves his facility, he should not do any such thing that makes him come back. He wants the captive to be reformed, and that makes him study the files intensely and channel the captives into the best program for their betterment.

Albert plays a huge role in the lives of all the captives who are under his wing. Most of them appreciate all that he does; and once free, many come by sometime to visit him at the facility. However, needless to say, these same convicts had hated him when they were inmates and he pushed them into specific programs for their betterment.

Albert is very proud of his free men who have regular jobs and earn their living honestly. He has pictures of them in a special folder with their current status and addresses. That folder is his trophy and he cherishes it. He always goes through it when he is feeling low or when a particular convict does not appreciate his kindness and is unpleasant to him. That folder is like a cane that helps him walk when the path in his life is hard and difficult.

He is actually browsing through the pages of that folder and munching on the grilled sandwich Amelia has made for him. It has stirred fried vegetables and pieces of bacon. Amelia has also packed a can of soda along with the sandwich. She knows her man very well.

The clock strikes 12 just as he finishes the last bite of his sandwich. He clears his table by throwing away the wrapper of the sandwich in the bin and keeping the soda aside. He puts away his precious folder in the drawer. He knows this is a testing time for his patience and says a little prayer to calm himself while taking deep breathes.

There is a knock on his door. Albert shouts, "Come in" and gets up from his chair. He is expecting Dr. Beringer, and has been waiting for him to come since the morning, even though he knew he would come at noon.

Dr. Beringer enters, shuts the door and sits down. He is in an awful state, wearing wrinkled clothes and looks really tired as if he has spent a sleepless night. Albert notices it, but does not comment on his appearance. Instead, he taps on his desk and asks, "So, Robert do you have the report for me?"

Robert has a file in his hand. He places it on the desk and slides it towards his boss with trembling hands and waits for Mateo to question him with regards to his report.

Albert opens the folder and starts reviewing the papers. His facial expressions which were calm when he started reading change, his eyebrows rise, he pauses, takes a couple of deep breaths as his brow furrows and his hand goes to his forehead as though trying to rub the creases that form on it. He closes the folder, joins his hands and put them under his chin, while looking at Robert and rocking his chair.

"So, Ricardo the convict came to Peter asking for Amphetamine drug and when he was refused, he threatened Peter with a scalpel around his neck saying that he has connections and Peter's life would be in danger."

Robert nods, "I even saw a small mark on Peter's neck from the scalpel. Fortunately Peter got away on time. The threat really scared him and he called out to the guards who took Ricardo back to his cell.

When I arrived, Peter told me all about it. He was trembling and was insisting on resigning. I tried to soothe him and said that all convicts say that they have connections so, don't worry. After that I went to see a patient."

Albert nods, "Anyone would feel scared when threatened and attacked physically. But, all convicts threaten that they have connections. So, what made him write a resignation letter and slide it under my door instead of talking to me?"

Robert says, "Later that evening, Peter got an anonymous phone call. The caller knew everything that happened between him and Ricardo and threatened him with consequences. Peter was scared and he interrupted my visit to the patient told me about it. He also told me that he had written his resignation and slid it under your office door."

A deeply disturbed Albert gets up from his chair, "So, your report indicates that the anonymous call was tracked to the main kitchen of our facility. This is disturbing. Who is this person and how could he enter our facility? Why did he make a call? A personal threat would have made a deeper impact."

Robert says, "Sure, but then Peter would have seen his face and could have identified him?"

Albert nods and mumbles, "I hope this anonymous caller is an outsider and not one of our employees."

Robert whispers, "I fear the same thing. I have heard bad things about mafia gangs. My parents still live in fear of them and have stopped visiting our hometown in Italy. If this person works in our institution then we all are doomed. We have to let go of this convict before anyone gets killed."

Albert can sense his fear and tries to pacify him, "Don't worry Robert. My past also involves countering corrupt officials who grabbed my ancestral land and shut down my once flourishing fishing business that employed many needy people. I have seen the worst."

Robert was shocked to hear this and wanted more details.

Albert let it all out with the hope that he will get closure on that chapter of his life, which also took his parents away from him, and not a day goes by that he doesn't feel a sense of frustration with his destiny, for he loved what he used to do in Portugal.

There was a pause in the room.

Then after a deep breathe, Albert continues, "I will call a meeting of all the head officials of all the departments and ask them to give me a list of new employees with their backgrounds. If this anonymous caller is from our facility, he will be tracked down in no time. I notice that as per your report, Ricardo, the convict has come into our facility just a month back. You take the day off, you look tired."

Albert's confidence is in complete contrast to Robert's tension. Robert removes his glasses and puts them in the pocket of his lab coat. His eyes are twitching with strain, and he wants to say more but Albert forestalls this. "Your fear can be sensed from 2 feet. Why don't you get a hold on it before it spreads? Take the day off. Your assistant, Joseph can take care of issues in your absence."

He waves him away, and as he turns, he adds, "Oh, and another thing. I will be emailing Peter that his resignation has not been accepted and he can and should resume his duties soon. I'll mark you in the copy."

Robert nods and leaves, stopping by at his department to update his assistant, Dr. Stone about his leave for the day.

Dr. Joseph Stone is a young graduate from the UCLA medical school, full of energy and always ready to take up any challenges and duties. He is making notes of some of the in-house patients he had seen in the morning, and preparing the report he has to hand over to Dr. Beringer every evening.

Dr. Beringer barges in and says, "Joseph I am not feeling well. I feel I am coming down with something. I am leaving early and have informed Albert."

"Sure, not a problem. I'll continue with the patients and submit all my reports tomorrow." Joseph says.

Robert taps on his desk as if trying to cut short his reply, "Make sure you attend the meeting in the evening with Albert. You will be representing our department. Ask Leon to be around in case of any emergencies."

Leon is their intern nurse. He is funny and young. Joseph and Leon have a great camaraderie and some convicts like it as they create a light and jovial atmosphere around them.

Joseph nods and Robert turns to his office to go get his car keys. Joseph calls after him, "Hope you feel better, Doc."

Robert waves and says, "Yay, yay sure. Thanks!"

Eight

Amelia wakes up after her afternoon siesta, and checks the time. It's 3pm and she freshens up and goes to her son's room, wanting to tidy it up before his friend comes to hand him his schoolwork.

Leonardo is listening to some music with his headphones on his ears. He removes them and asks, "Mom what are you doing?"

"Aren't you expecting company, Leonardo?"

"Yeah, sure mom. But, please don't do this. I have to look like a regular teen."

Mom looks at him and starts laughing, "Sure, I understand."

She leaves his shirt hanging on his chair. Just then she hears the doorbell ring. She goes to Leonardo to straighten his collar but he protests, so, she ruffles his hair and goes to the door.

There are three teenagers outside the door, one of them tucking his shirt in, and tidying himself while the other two observe him in confusion.

Amelia opens the door and introduces herself. The three teenagers greet her and tell her they are Steve, Daren and Katie, Leonardo's classmates. Katie has a bunch of papers in her hand. She gestures them to come in and shows them Leonardo's bedroom, and gets them chairs. Leonardo is sitting up and anxiously greets them, as they have visited him for the first time at his home. He has practiced saying *Hi, what's up?* Many times while his mom was taking a nap. He's pretty certain he has mastered it, but when his friends enter the room, he is jubilant seeing them and waves, but his words don't come out.

The three of them individually shake his hand and then sit down. Amelia goes to the kitchen to get them some hot chocolate while straining her ears to overhear their conversation. Initially she could hear some voices, which then fade away. This happened repeatedly until she took in the hot chocolate. Once the beverages were served, the conversation loosened up. Amelia could hear lots of laughter and continuous talk that carried into the kitchen, where she had started preparing dinner, beef stew with brown rice, which both her boys love. They both deserved a special treat.

While stirring the pot, she dials Albert's cell number, which goes unanswered. Assuming that he is in a meeting she hangs up. After a few minutes the phone beeps and she receives a text from him, "In a meeting, will call later. Love"

She smiles and texts him back, "No problem, good luck. I will wait up patiently to hear from you. Much love."

Leonardo is getting briefed up over his new classes, his professors and the assignments. Steve asks him if he is getting overwhelmed, but Leonardo seemed overjoyed, "No man, I am excited. Finally I get to do some constructive work." His three friends chuckle, while Daren comments, "So typical of you, dude."

Steve and Daren get up, shake hands with him and take the 4 cups outside.

Katie is searching something in her bag and finally finds it. She gets up and gives that special envelope to Leonardo saying, "This is for you."

Leonardo frowns, "What is this and who is it from?"

Katie whispers in his ear, "Sophia"

Leonardo blushes and quickly puts it on the other side of the bed.

Katie notices his reaction and taps his shoulder lightly, "She likes you Leonardo and wants to come by. I did not know how you would take that, so this card."

Leonardo tries to act normal and replies, "Sure, she can come by anytime. Friends are always welcome."

Katie smiles, "Okay then she will come along with me tomorrow."

Leonardo gulps with excitement. He wants to shout *yeah* but instead says, "Oh ok. That will be fun. Oh, by the way do thank her for the card."

Katie starts heading out of the room, smiles and replies, "You could do that yourself tomorrow."

The teens thank Mrs. Silva and head out. She thanks them for coming by.

Shutting the door after them, she puts the stove on simmer and goes into Leonardo's room, and sees Leonardo staring at the envelope.
"What is that, Leonardo?"

"Oh, nothing mom." He shrugs and put the envelope aside. "Nothing at all."

Amelia senses something fishy but lets it slide. She changes the topic by asking about school and assignments.

Leonardo relaxes and they converse. She asks if he would like to see some television. He refuses saying that he should start on his studies.

Amelia agrees and leaves the room.

Leonardo picks up the envelope again and opens it to see a beautiful *Get Well Soon* card, with simple words penned on it,

Get Well soon cause I miss you!

Best wishes,

Sophia.

Leonardo stares at the words and feels a warm gush

of blood flow through his body. He had always wondered how he would feel if he ever had a crush, and this was his first time. He was on the top of the world. He had never thought that liking someone would make a person feel so satisfied and content as if nothing else matters in the world.

He wants to keep her card on his side table as an incentive to heal faster, but then realizes his parents will have a hundred questions for him. So he slides it under his pillow, hoping that this will give him sweet dreams that night.

He starts working on his assignment, but that card is very distracting and he keeps sliding his hand under the pillow to touch it to make sure it is there, as though it will vanish away in thin air.

****

Albert is conducting the meeting at the facility, and updates his officials about the incident and asks all the heads to give him a list of all the recently hired employees who have been working in the facility for just 2-3 months, along with their respective background. He also asks for information about the 'temps' or temporary workers. He wants to get into the bottom of this anonymous threat.

Another meeting is scheduled for the next day at 1 p.m. for all the officials to bring in the lists for scrutiny and action.

Once they leave the room, he pings his secretary and informs her about the next meeting, relaxes in his chair with a cup of coffee and calls up his wife.

He does not give her details but just tells her that things are fine and he will be home on time. He inquires about Leonardo and hangs up the phone.

Amelia is relieved to know that and thanks the spirits for guiding the Silva family.

Dinner is ready, and she goes to check in on Leonardo, who is supposedly working on his assignments. She enters abruptly and catches him in the 'act'. His hand is under the pillow. She's curious and raises her eyebrows at the weird position he is in and stands there waiting for him to explain his weird behavior. Leonardo blushes as he quietly pulls out the card from under the pillow and hands it to her.

Amelia takes the card and sits on the chair next to him. The front of the card has a teddy bear on it. She opens the card and reads it and cannot help laughing loudly as she gets up to hug her son. She is so happy to see this card, they always wanted their son to live a normal life, have crushes like a normal teen. Leonardo is confused by her behavior, "Mom, why are you laughing?"

"I am just happy that you get to feel these emotions in your life. Isn't it just out the world? It's wonderful isn't it, how you can feel so powerful yet handicapped at the same time."

Leonardo agrees, "Actually, yes mom. I am confused yet elated at this feeling. Why do such feelings erupt? I just like that person and yet so many emotions are evolving out of it, already."

Amelia agrees, "This is what the attraction is all about, my son. When both people like each other, there is a mutual chemistry, which is effortless and can even turn into a true romance. Now, I don't mean to scare you over commitment issues right now, it's too early. That's how your dad and I met. We were high school sweethearts who parted ways to test our love but then we were destined to be together." She speaks with pride.

Leonardo is still confused and hesitant but for the moment is right, he asks his question, "Mom, I was just eyeing her from a distance and all of a sudden this fondness for her, does not look normal. I mean, I have not even kissed her or anything and already I have this feeling that she is precious to me and there is not even a bit of lust in it." He hesitates a moment and then adds, "Yet"

"I understand all these feelings, son. I am so happy that you came to me with these issues especially since this is your first time."

"Excuse me mom, you caught me in the act. I did not come up to you." Leonardo interjects.

Amelia agrees, "I thank my timing for it." She winks and continues, "But with time, you will know what to do and how to channel your feelings. If you feel you are attracted to her and she to you, then go for it. Spend time together; get to know each other. However; make sure you focus on your goal in life especially since this is your crucial year."

Leonardo agrees and hugs her back, "Thanks mom, for being who you are and always supporting me."

"I love you son" and she kisses his forehead.

Leonardo is goal orientated and always connects closely to his parents for guidance. They appreciate his diligence but want him to enjoy his youth and the perks, which came along with it. They emigrated from Portugal with the intention to give their kid the best.

The doorbell rings, Amelia goes to open it. It is Albert, she hugs him and he kisses her and enters the living room calling for Leonardo, "How's it going son?"

Leonardo shouts back, as he shoves the card back under the pillow, "Great dad, how're you doing?"

Albert walks into his room and Leonardo extends his hand to his dad. They shake hands like adults and then Albert ruffles his son's hair fondly.

Leonardo smiles as he enjoys this gesture of affection.

Amelia comes in with a bottle of beer for Albert.

Albert sits down next to Leonardo and sees his books spread all over the bed. He realizes that Leonardo's friends had come down to give him his assignments and is happy for him.

Amelia could hear the two chat as she started heating the dinner. She laid out the dinner plates on the table, which was in one corner of the living room. She hopes that Leonardo shows that card to his dad. It would thrill him.

She faintly hears Leonardo's voice followed by Albert's louder one. Her heart skips a beat as she tries to eavesdrop on their conversation. After a while, she gives up all pretenses and walks into Leonardo's room where she sees Albert sitting on the bed next to Leonardo, hugging him. He has the card in his hand. She was so happy to see that scene that her eyes get teary. Unwilling to interrupt the father and son bonding she turns around to go, but Leonardo shouts, "Mom, dad is teasing me. Please ask him to quit it."

She grins, as she likes such situations where she has to take control of her family. Turning, she puts her hands on her waist, and tells Albert "Okay, quit it."

Albert knows that she likes such situations so; he immediately takes his hands off his son's shoulder and raises them, "As you say, boss. I was just trying to have fun with our little kid who is not little anymore, I guess."

Amelia chokes up over it, "Sure, he is now going to date young girls and he has become a big boy."

Leonardo corrects her, "*Girl* mom not *Girls*."

Albert looks at her and winks, "His romance chemistry is already looking strong, my dear."

Amelia starts to laugh.

Leonardo is a little confused.

She then announces that dinner is ready. Albert goes to change his clothes, dropping the empty beer bottle in the recycling bin on his way to his room.

Amelia helps Leonardo to the washroom and then to the table. They enjoy a pleasant meal with lots of conversation and laughter, after which she clears the table while Albert helps Leonardo back to his room, and helps him change and clean up. Leonardo wants to sit at his desk for some serious study. The card is still lying on the bed. Leonardo asks, "Can I place it next to my night table?" Albert winks at him, "Atta boy!"

Albert goes out, shutting the door partially since he wants to watch TV and not disturb his son. Then he helps Amelia who is putting stuff in the dishwasher by cleaning the kitchen.
Once that is done, they sit on the couch close to each other while Albert turns on the television. This is Amelia's favorite moment, something she looks forward to the whole day.

She puts her head on his strong wide shoulder, "So what is your plan of action." She knows that Albert would have a plan and now wanted details.

Albert tells her about the meeting scheduled for the next day when he would get the reports of background checks made on new and temporary employees. He is optimistic that the anonymous caller would be caught.

Amelia says amen to that.

The clock strikes 9 p.m. and Amelia gets up to give Leonardo his medicines. Albert watches television for another hour while Amelia changes and reads for a while in bed.

The Silva parents call it a night, and Leonardo stays up late, studying. He is not as distracted about the card or Sophia's visit the next day, after confiding in his parents.

Nine

The next day, after sending off Leonardo to work, Amelia cleans whatever little mess the living room had been in. With Leonardo confined to his room, there is not much of a mess in the house except his room. She wants to clean Leonardo's room but he is deep asleep, so she postpones it. She takes a quick shower, dons her jeans and shirt and sprays some perfume. On her way to the kitchen, she hears some sound from Leonardo's room so she walks in. He is sitting up in his bed with his headphones on. She waves at him; he switches off the music and wishes her, "Good morning, Mom."

"How was your night, honey?"

"Good" replies Leonardo.

"What time did you sleep?" She asks

"Oh, around 1am" answers her son.

She sees the card on his bedside table and winks, "Hope you had sweet dreams."

Leonardo blushes and protests, "Mom!" Then he hesitates and admits, "Actually, I did. It feels nice that there is someone out there besides my parents who wishes for my welfare."

Amelia is touched by his honesty. She ruffles his hair and asks him if he needs help to go to the restroom. He nods.

Once he is freshened up, he ensures that he wears extra cool clothes since he is expecting someone special in the evening. Amelia helps him to the dining table, and serves him breakfast.

"Did dad leave for work, mom?"

"Yes, honey. He did. He will call you later to speak to you."

"Okay, no problem." Leonardo replies while pouring syrup over his pancakes. He enjoys a stack of pancakes with lots of syrup over it. Amelia fusses over him and ensures that he has 2 boiled eggs after his pancakes, followed by a cup of milk, to balance all the carbs. He's a growing kid whose metabolism is at its peak and food is never an issue for him. From the kitchen, she asked him, "So, what do you want to eat for lunch?"

"Oh, anything that is not walking and is cooked." He jokes.

Amelia chuckles, Leonardo is not a picky eater; and can eat anything that is cooked and served on a plate.

She starts to boil enough pasta that would suffice for both lunch and dinner.

Leonardo finishes his breakfast and gulps down his medicines with a glass of water.

Amelia helps him to his room, and he settles down to listen to some music before resuming his schoolwork. Amelia has no issues, since he never shirked his work.

Albert reaches his facility and immediately takes a tour of all the entire facility to get a first hand report.

He walks into the kitchen where the assistants are busy exchanging a little laughter while doing their normal chores such as chopping vegetables, cleaning and scrubbing dishes. There are some convicts who are also scrubbing the pots, under the supervision of guards. The head cook is checking the day's menu while stirring the pot. He has to serve lunch in two hours time and then start with dinner.

Albert relaxes a bit and turns to go when he notices something unusual about a guard who was supervising one of the inmates. The guard takes something out of his pocket and gives it to the inmate, who swiftly hides it in his pocket. The guard looks around to make sure that no one has seen them in this act.

Albert frowns as he studies the behavior of the inmate and the guard, who have not exchanged a word, just communicated through gestures and eye contact. With great effort he controls his desire to apprehend the criminal immediately and pull out the stuff from his pocket. He notes the number of the captive, which is sewn on his uniform. He then goes to the guards' office. The head guard, John Kemp is at his table revising the details of recent employees, which was required for noon's meeting He looks up, sees Albert standing at his desk, and gets up to greet him. Albert shakes hands with John, who gestures the warden to take a seat.

Officer John Kemp has been the head of the guards for over a decade now and he is as efficient as Warden Silva. The guards look up to him and do not question his decisions as he is logical and looks after their interests.

Albert sits down and comes straight to the point, "John, could you please look into your log and tell me the name of the guard responsible for convict no. 457?"

"Sure, Albert" saying that he turns towards the computer to open the appropriate file. He has many questions for his warden, knows it's not the right time to ask them now.
"Did you say, 457 Albert?" John wants to be sure before he uttered the guard's name.

"Yes!" Replied Albert

"His name is Javier, and he got employed in our facility two weeks back. In fact, I have put his name in my sheet, where his background is also given." He begins to read the details from his sheet. Albert interrupts him, certain that he has found the culprit, "Page him to come here, right now. Also ask some of the guards to arrest him as soon as he comes to your office. I want this man in my office for questioning."

John looks puzzled, but does not say anything as Albert continues, "Ask another set of guards to go to convict 457 and search him and his cell."

John feels a surge of adrenaline in him, gets up and says, "Yes, sir."

Albert gets up, nodded and started walking to his office. His steps are steady and he is walking tall with confidence, as if he had just won a battle over the fear and agony that tormented many in this facility. He thought about Peter and murmured, "Wish he would come back."

It is half past eleven and Albert knows that the officials would be coming to his office in another thirty minutes for the meeting. He is confident he had nabbed the right person and wants to update his co-workers once the matter is completely investigated. He pages his secretary Peggy, "Please cancel my noon appointment and reschedule it for 5pm."

Peggy senses some excitement in his voice, and re-confirms it, "So, you want to cancel your appoint and what, sir?"

Albert pauses, "Yes, Peggy please cancel it and reschedule it for 5p.m. instead."

"Reason, sir" questions Peggy.

Albert becomes a little impatient, but, realizing that he had given the red code for this meeting due to its importance, he should explain his reason for re-scheduling it. He replies, "Inform them that something has come up related to that issue and I have had to postpone the meeting till 5p.m."

Peggy, finding the answer reasonable, hung up.

In no time, there was a knock on his door. Mateo and two other guards escort the new employee, Javier into the room.

Albert asks Javier to be seated and signals the rest of the guards including Mateo to stand around him. Albert sits facing, and stares at him sternly; giving him an unspoken message that he knows what he is up to.

Javier puts on a confident demeanor, which Albert senses immediately and changes his strategy.

"Hi Javier, how have you been?"

"Good" Javier responds, cool outwardly, playing with his silver bracelet. He is terrified but does not want to show it.

Albert comes to the point quickly, "Javier, today I saw you give something to convict no. 457. It was a small package, which he put it in his pocket. Would you like to share with me the contents of that packet?"

Javier's eyes pop out. Until now, he was quite confident that no one saw that act. He tries to feign ignorance as he mutters, "What packet? I don't know what you are talking about." He ends the sentence with a sly laugh.

John enters with a brown bag, without knocking and places the packet on Albert's desk. Albert. Albert pierces it with his letter opener and sticks his finger into it and brings it out, coated with white powder, sniffs it and licks it slightly. It is definitely some form of drug. He pages Dr. Beringer. Dr. Beringer does not want to come, but his boss's commands forces him to walk towards his office.

Dr. Beringer takes ten minutes to come and in the meantime, Albert is questioning and threatening Javier about the contents of the packet. His words are stern and capable of making the guilty very scared. The past ten years had made him an expert at this, and given an outlet for the anger at the corrupt officials who took away his ancestral land which made him leave his homeland and dream job. Javier is sweating profusely and he confesses, " I don't know what it is but I was told to give it to Ricardo."

Albert and John both ask together, "Told?"

"So there is more to it?" Albert muttered rubbing his forehead.

"Why are you supplying Ricardo with this drug? What is the benefit of it to you?" Albert leans towards Javier and asks, his eyes blood red, and his voice stern.

Javier shudders and confesses, "The goal is to make people addicts in this facility and hamper their progress in their individual programs so that you don't get the success you have been getting so far."

Albert starts to laugh bitterly as if he was spitting venom. He just did not understand why someone would be against him. He was doing something for the betterment of the community and "someone" out there wanted to destroy everything good.

John empathizes with him and puts his hand on Albert's shoulder as if trying to console him. Mateo feels sorry for the warden and is also angry with this 'someone' who is targeting his boss and harming the program that will help many convicts to get to lead a good life.

Dr. Beringer comes in and sees Javier sitting with his head down surrounded by guards. In one corner of the room Albert and John are standing close to each other. He spots the brown bag on the table, and he stretches his hand with the thought that he should just pick it up and head out.

Albert sees him and walks towards him, "Hi Robert, how have you been?"

Robert nods as if to say fine but not fine seeing this scene.

Albert points to the brown bag, "I want this bag to be investigated in about an hour's time. Can this be done, Dr. Beringer?"

Dr. Beringer nods, "Sure, warden."

Javier looks up and Dr. Beringer gets uncomfortable and wants to get away as soon as possible. He picks up the bag and leaves. Once outside, he takes a deep breath, and continues walking towards his clinic.

Albert goes and stands near Javier. He yanks his hair viciously and says in a cold angry voice, "I want to know the name of this someone."

Javier tries to force his head down and cries loudly, "Please sir, I can't say his name. He will kill me. I can't tell. I am sorry."

Mateo slaps his shoulder from one side, "You have to tell us the name or else, you will get killed here."

Mateo is a fearless and dedicated guard, who does not care that he is risking his toddler's future and his responsibilities towards his new family.
Albert appreciates his dedication and pats his shoulder, as if to pacify him. Then he orders Mateo and the other guards to put Javier in an isolated cell to give him enough time to rationalize between what is right and wrong and come up with the name. The guards force Javier up and start walking towards the cell.

Albert sits down on his chair. John comes to sit across him. They look at each other coming to terms with what they have learnt. Someone has an agenda of personal vengeance. In another hour's time, the officials of the various departments are to assemble. He has data to inform them and Dr. Beringer's results would be in by then. He hopes to get tips and ideas from other departments to crack this thing. John excuses himself saying, "I will join in at 5p.m. with the others."

Albert steps out to take a walk in the open grounds, deep in thought. He considers quitting the post as a warden, so that the personal vengeance would not curb the progress of his convicts who had a chance of becoming good citizens. Just then his cell phone rings.

He answers it in a pensive voice. It is Leonardo. "Hello, dad, is that you?"

Albert says in a much more cheerful tone, "Hi Leonardo. How have you been, son?"

Leonardo says in concern, "What happened dad. Your voice did not sound like you at all. Are you okay?"

Albert is tempted to break down and tell him the whole story. But instead he gathers his courage, "I am fine, son. I was just thinking about something and my phone rang. How are you feeling, today? Sorry I could not call you earlier during the day."

"That's all right Dad. I am doing much better, getting stronger hour by hour."

"That's good to hear, Leonardo. I hope you get well and get back to your routine."

Albert forgets that today Leonardo's special friend will come by to meet him, but is reminded by Leonardo.

"I don't mind staying in this position for some time, Dad. I am getting pampered by Mom and my friends who visit me every evening, and today my special friend is going to come by."

Albert tries hard to remember his special friend's name, but stress is affecting his memory.

Leonardo continues, "So Dad, what time do I see you in the evening?"

"Son, I have a meeting at 5p.m. and don't know how long it will last. In fact you both should have dinner, and not wait up for me."

Leonardo senses some trouble, and said, "Okay dad, hold on. Mom wants to speak to you."

Putting the phone on mute, he calls Amelia and tells her about Albert's strained voice and about him coming later today.

She frowns, takes the phone and walked out to the living room and says, "Hi honey, how are you?"

Albert melts at the sound of her voice. Gone is the stern warden of the correctional facility, he is just a man in need of her care.

He wants to blurt out all that happened but cannot do that over that phone. So he just says, "Hi, I am okay. I have a crucial meeting in another forty minutes where we will make some worthy decisions for this facility."

Amelia wants to sound positive, "Okay. That's good to hear, honey. I am sure you will stay focused on the situation and make a wise decision. I will wait up for you at home over dinner."

"No Amelia. Please have your dinner on time. I am pretty sure, I will be late, honey."

Amelia replies calmly, "Sure, honey as you say."

She senses Albert is not in the mood to talk further, so she ends the conversation, "Good luck Albert. I am sure the guided spirits will help you through this time. My best wishes are with you."

Albert closes his eyes and murmurs softly, "Amen" and disconnects the call.

Amelia puts the phone to her chest and said a prayer.

There's a knock at the door followed by the doorbell. She gets up and opens it, and lets in Katie, Daren and another girl, who she presumes is Sophia. She introduces herself to Sophia and greets all of them, and ushers them in.

She announces their arrival to Leonardo from the living room so that he can straighten himself out, while she directs them to his room. Daren helps Amelia with the chairs while the girls step into Leonardo's room.

Leonardo's face brightens as he sees them. He's blushing hard and his body is radiating warmth. Becoming conscious of it, he puts his head down and tries to take a few deep breaths to try and be normal.

Sophia goes to his bed and extends her hand, "Hi Leonardo, how are you doing?"

Leonardo looks up, trying to be very calm but his heart is beating fast and he can hear it flutter. So his response is over enthusiastic, "I am good, thanks!"

Amelia and Daren bring in the chairs. Katie gestures Sophia to sit next to the bed while she and Daren sit next to her.

Katie tells Amelia, "Mrs. Silva, Daren and I have to leave early so, please don't bother about giving us something to drink."

"Sure, thanks for informing me Katie," replies Amelia and heads to the kitchen.

Daren has brought some papers and Katie prompts him to give those to Leonardo so that they can go, and Sophia and Leonardo can get some time alone.

Daren has a smirk on his face, and asks Leonardo, "Hey dude, how is it going?" Leonardo and he high five and Daren ruffles his hair. Daren tells him what is happening at school and shows him the other assignments due next week. Leonardo nods trying to understand it all. He hands his completed assignments to Daren to deliver to the teachers. Daren browses through them and says, "Wow, you have aced this one."

Leonardo grins, "Thanks!"

Amelia brings in two cups of hot cocoa. Sophia takes a cup and Leonardo takes the other.

Daren and Katie get up with the pretext that they have their assignment deadlines to meet and promise to come next day. While leaving, Katie shares an amusing incident about their Chemistry professor and his funny accent, which makes everyone go in splits of laughter.

Amelia shuts the door behind them, tempted for a moment to re-enter Leonardo's room but realizes that they should be left alone to bond and know each other. She goes into the kitchen, physically preparing dinner but mentally with Albert in his office.

In Leonardo's room, there is an awkward silence initially. Then Sophia breaks the ice by gesturing to the card on his side table, "So, you liked the card?"

"Oh yes, thanks for the card and the lines were touching." He smiles genuinely.

"You are welcome!" said Sophia.

There is silence again while both sip their beverages. This time Leonardo initiates the conversation, "So, how is school? What do you plan to major in?"

"I intend to get my bachelor's in English literature and hope that I fare well in my required courses. Unfortunately, I can't escape them," she says jokingly.

Leonardo joins in the laughter, "Oh yeah, got to do what they ask from us. No choice, huh."

"So, senior year now and you must have got all your pre-requisites and school finalized. You are known for that in our school. This must have given you more time to start preparing for it."
"Yes, I have it all sorted out." Leonardo answers. This is his favorite topic and he can talk for hours on it. He starts talking and pauses every now and then to ask her, "I hope I am not boring you."

Sophia smiles and encourages him, "No, not at all. I like how you get all fascinated about your future."

Leonardo blushes and explains, "Sophia, I immigrated to this country when I was five years old. I have seen how my parents earn each dollar since we came empty handed from our home in Portugal. This makes me more determined to be a professional so that I can give them a comfortable life, which they deserve. Luckily, I won't have to move a lot. With Silicon Valley nearby, I can get a job there and still continue to live near my parents."

Sophia puts her hand on his shoulder, "I am sure they must be so proud of you, Leonardo."

That touch makes Leonardo fluster and pause mid sentence, forgetting what to say. He is blank but was also quite happy with the present situation. He has only one wish in his life, to be a software professional. Now, however, he has gradually started hoping for another wish in his life, and she was sitting right in front of him.

Amelia has finished making dinner and decides that the two teens need to part and go their way. She enters his room wearing a smile, "Hello kids" she announces while entering so that they can stop any conversation that was not meant for her ears. Both of them look at her.

Leonardo greets her back, "Hey mom"

She sits on one of the chairs and although the scene is a little uncomfortable, she tries to make conversation, "So, Sophia I hear you are a junior?"

"Yes, Mrs. Silva" she replies

"Oh great. You could take Leonardo's last year's notes. They will help you."

Leonardo agrees, "Sure mom she could on some courses since I plan on majoring in Science. She intends to major in English Literature."

"Oh English Literature" exclaims Amelia.

"I am also an English Literature major. What a coincidence, Sophia."

Sophia chuckles, "Wow, it sure is." She likes how Leonardo's mom was trying to be friendly to her.

"So, where do you live, Sophia?"

"I live just another bus stop away from here." Saying that she pulls out her cell phone from her purse and looked at the time.

"Oh wow, it is past 6p.m. I should get going."

Amelia gets up, picks up those two cups and heads out. She knows that the kids need some time alone to say their byes. Her mind returns repeatedly to her husband's meeting and hopes that everything works out for the best.

Leonardo sees Sophia's phone and suggests with a little bit of hesitation, "So, could we stay in touch via phone calls?"

"Absolutely," agrees Sophia.

She asks for his number and starts to dial it, and once it rings, she hangs up. "There we both have each other's number now."

She winks and says, "Call me, maybe."

Leonardo laughs, "Sure"

Sophia waves, steps out and thanks Amelia for the hot cup of chocolate.

"Oh, you are very welcome, dear." Amelia replies without hesitation.

Sophia likes his mom, already, she finds her very friendly and grounded.

After shutting the door, Amelia rushes to Leonardo's room with wide eyes and a huge smile, "So, how was it, sonny boy? Details, details, details."

She sits down next to him and tries to tickle his tummy.

Leonardo has his cell phone in his hand and is saving her number. He is a little embarrassed by his parent's excitement, but starts telling her. Amelia listens quietly without making any judgments. When Leonardo finishes talking about it, she looks delighted and satisfied with his approach.

Leonardo also updates her about his latest assignment and was wondering if he can go to school next week to submit it personally since it requires an oral presentation as well.

Amelia thinks that it could be done if she drove him back and forth. She, however, thinks she should consult the doctor before making such a decision. Saying that, she gets up to go, and the mask falls from her face and her worry for her husband shows. Leonardo sees it and shouts after her, "Mom" She turns back and he says, "Dad will be back in time for dinner. In fact, we will have it together. Let's wait up for him." He has a smile on his face.

Amelia's eyes fill up with tears. She nods and leaves the room before she breaks down and creates a scene. She goes into the backyard under the pretext of taking a stroll. While walking her mind is busy thinking how remarkable fate is and that whatever happens in everybody's life has a reason for it. If they had left their hometown in such a devastated state, Leonardo would not have realized how tough life is, and how much his parents had suffered to provide shelter and food for him in this new country. If Albert's ancestral land would not have been seized by corrupt officials, they would have been living a very comfortable life and Leonardo would not have got exposed to what the real hardships are and may not have had the respect he has for his parents.

She is confident in their destiny and knows that fate had a bright future for them even though her husband at times doubted it.

It has started to get chilly. California usually gets a little cold during the early winters, so she comes into the house, sits on the couch and starts to knit her half done muffler. Her thoughts usually give her company when she is alone. While her fingers are working on the scarf, her mind is miles away. The clock strikes 7, she glances at it and continues knitting.

At half past seven the doorbell rings. Confident that it is her husband she calls enthusiastically, "Coming" and puts her knitting away in its bag. She opens the door sees Albert who has a huge smile on his face. Amelia hugs him.

Leonardo shouts from his room, "Hi Dad"

Albert shouts back, "Hey son, how is it going?" Amelia whispers into his ear, "Sophia was here this evening." Albert frowns and Amelia whispers again, "His friend, Sophia, who gave that card."

Albert nods, "Got it, thanks dear."

Amelia and Albert went into Leonardo's room together hand in hand. Albert starts teasing Leonardo about his special friend and his son takes it in a good stride. Amelia sees all this and smiles to see her happy family. She gets up to get her husband a bottle of beer and starts heating up the pasta and grilling the garlic bread. The garlic creates an appetizing aroma. Both the father and son came out instantly on the table.

Amelia was laying the table and was surprised to see them even before she called them.

Albert does not bother to change, and they sit down and enjoy their dinner amidst warmth and laughter. While the boys are teasing each other, Amelia looks at Albert to see if his smile and laughter are genuine which would give her a clue as to how his day went. She is happy to see that his smile is genuine and is looking forward to her comfortable moment on the couch with her hubby.

Dishes done, son settled in, the couple sat on their couch in their favorite position and Albert gives her an overview of his day.

"The meeting was remarkable, Amelia. I offered to resign because the convicts future could get into trouble by this personal vengeance."

Amelia was confused and asked him to clarify what he meant by personal vengeance.

Albert realizes that she is unaware of the latest developments and tells her about the incident of Javier and how he was caught giving a packet to a convict and when confronted, he confessed that someone had asked him to do that so that the warden does not succeed in working for the betterment of the convicts.

Amelia's jaw drops as she wonders who that person is.

Albert taps her shoulder and continues, "So my colleagues did not accept it and said that we all will tackle it together. Javier will be in the lockup until he gives out the name of that person who wants me to suffer."

Amelia is happy about the result but also upset that Albert had considered taking such a big decision like resignation without discussing with her.

Albert hugs her tightly and confides, "I am sorry, I did not inform you of this big decision but it all happened so quickly. Javier was detected by chance and when he mentioned this other person, I did not think about myself but of my convicts whom I work for. How could I put their future into jeopardy and be selfish?"

Amelia gets emotional and kisses him, "Mr. Silva you are a good man. I am proud of you."

Albert kisses her back saying, "I know that Mrs. Silva and you make me a better person."

They both start laughing while still hugging each other. There is a twinkle in Amelia's eye. Albert started caressing her breast affectionately. Amelia pushes him away with a giggle.

Just then the clock strikes nine and Amelia gets up to give Leonardo his medicines, after which she changes and settles in bed with a book.

Albert comes in unusually early and they make love. Albert sleeps like a baby, leaving Amelia wide awake as she realizes how hungry she was for his love and she felt light as a feather as all her tensions and stress were wiped away.

Ten

The next morning was the usual affair of Albert going for a jog and then leaving early after breakfast determined to break Javier's silence. Amelia can read his mind and wishes him luck.

She takes a shower before Leonardo wakes up and then has breakfast with him. After breakfast she calls his doctor to make an appointment for his check up and gets a slot for a noon appointment.

She tells Leonardo about the appointment and starts collecting all the X-rays, paperwork, and prescriptions so that they don't miss anything important. They decide to have lunch outside after their appointment so Amelia finishes the preliminary preparations for dinner, while Leonardo is trying to groom himself to his best of capacity.

They get to the hospital in time and Nurse Mary greets them and directs them to a room where she removes Leonardo's bandages and then asks them to wait until the doctor arrives. Leonardo is a little nervous and fidgety and Amelia checks her bag to ensure she had all the essential paperwork.

Dr. Henry enters after knocking and after the initial pleasantries he asks, "How have you been, young boy?"

Leonardo says with a smile, "I am doing excellent, Doc. Would you like to check my movements?"

The doctor had been practicing for over 8 years, and had seen many such zealous patients in his life wanting to go back to their normal lives. He likes his assertiveness and nods, "Sure, Leonardo after my check up if I feel that you are fine, you can presume your normal activities." He said with a smile.

After his examination he says, "Leonardo, you have made remarkable progress. I don't know how it happened, but you are much better today and your strength is coming back. You can start your physical therapy and also resume school for maybe 2-3 hours until your next check up."

Leonardo smiles happily and said with enthusiasm but softly, "Yes!" Amelia smiles at the doctor and says, "Thank you"

Dr. Henry pages his nurse and asks her to give them the names of therapists near their zip code. He wishes his patient good luck and asks Amelia to check back with them after a week.

The nurse puts the compression bandage, she demonstrates how to put it on and remove it so that Amelia can do it at home. She also hands Leonardo a pair of crutches since he is strong enough to go places on his own and ensures that he knows how to use them correctly.

After taking Leonardo's prescription, the list of therapists, and making a follow up appointment for the coming week, Amelia hugs Leonardo tight and jokes loudly, "I bet someone special sent good wishes for your speedy recovery."

Nurse Mary looks up. Leonardo does not get it the first time but then he knows where this is going and he asks her to quit it.

Amelia realizes that it is not appropriate so she backs off.

They lunched at a local burger joint indulging in burgers, fries and shakes. It is a fun filled afternoon especially with the news of his recovery. Amelia dials Albert and shares the good news with him. He is thrilled.

****

Javier had still not confessed the name in spite of all the pressure and torture. Albert is unhappy with the result, and is growing concerned. He has raised the number of guards on duty for each hour so that rigorous vigil will discourage bullies from entering the facility. He is grateful that the heads of all departments have not accepted his resignation and is even more motivated to keep them and the facility safe.

Amelia reminds him that he has been through even tougher times and this too shall pass. Albert agrees with her and disconnects the phone.

Leonardo is too excited after the meal and asks his mom if they should stop by his school for an hour or so. Amelia is skeptical about it but gives in to her son's persistence and drives him to school. Leonardo pulls down his window and takes deep breaths. He has missed school so much and wants each cell of his body to inhale these buildings and the atmosphere. She chuckles at his behavior.

She parks in the parking lot and asks him if she should help him to his class, so that he can collect the homework from his friends and save them a trip in the evening.

Leonardo likes the idea. He calls up his friend, Daren who is in the cafeteria and they decide to meet half way. Daren is happy to see him and takes out the sheets for Leonardo. Leonardo confirms that he will be present for the coming week's presentation and asks him to inform the professor about it. Daren is enthusiastic about it, "Great, all the classmates will be overjoyed to see you back in action."

Leonardo corrects him, "No, I will not get to play basketball for another month or so, but at least I can come back to school and join in the fun."

Leonardo is surprised to hear his own words. So much has changed for him in a week's time. His attitude towards life and how he defines fun is different now. He is happy now to just hang out with his classmates and share laughter.

After picking up medicines on the way, they drive home, where Leonardo rests a bit before attempting his homework. He has come to understand that he needs to take some time off. Amelia also takes a nap; supporting Leonardo's tall frame exhausts her.

Leonardo's cell phone rings, interrupting his nap. He is surprised but happy that it is Sophia. She wants to know how he is doing. He replies, "Hey, I am good. What a surprise." He sits up so that his voice does not betray too much of his excitement and continues, "Yeah, I am much better. In fact I picked up my notes from Daren while returning from my doc appointment to save him a trip to my home."

He pauses and adds, "Yeah, I am sorry for not coming by to meet you. I have been asked to take it easy and to walk only when necessary with crutches. But the good news is that I should be fine in no time and resume school. So, I will be meeting you soon." He blushes after uttering that sentence.

Amelia wakes up to the sound of the voices and peeps into Leonardo's room. Seeing that he is on the phone, she goes to the kitchen to make herself a cup of Joe and a hot chocolate for her son. While she was carrying the two cups to his room, she hears her son say bye and hang up.

Amelia enters, hands him the hot chocolate cup to sit down next to him. "So, who was it?" she asks casually.

Leonardo is still wearing a smile. Seeing that, she says, "Wait don't answer. I know who it was."

Leonardo blushes, but tells her about the conversation. She is conscious of the way he snapped her at the doctor's office and so is careful about her reaction.

They finish their beverages and she takes away the cups while he starts working on his assignments. He gets a few calls but now she was at ease and did not strain her ears to his conversations.

She makes a few phone calls and finalizes a therapist who works close to their home and also takes their insurance. He would begin from the next day. Then she settles down in the backyard, knitting her scarf and again wandering off miles away. This is her favorite past time and she loves it. When it is past six in the evening she started to bake the dough in the oven, while chopping vegetables, meat and putting them in separate dishes. Pizza is on the menu, a fairly easy preparation if the ingredients are chopped and kept ready.

Albert calls asking Amelia if he can pick up anything on his way home. She looks in the fridge and sees that they're out of beer and tells him. Albert arrives with a six-pack of beer, takes one bottle and sits down to chat with Leonardo while Amelia is busy in the kitchen.

Dinner is the usual affair of teasing and laughter but Amelia is cautious since she does not want Leonardo to snap at his father. She knows her son has high regard for his dad, but being young, he can be hot headed and say things without thinking.

Later, on their favorite couch, he updates her on Javier's silence but assures her that things seem normal in the facility. Even Peter the nurse has joined back.

Amelia is happy, but concerned about that 'someone' who dared to hamper her husband's work and hopes that he gets arrested soon. Albert reads her thoughts and says, "Amen"

They bring their heads together and chuckle softly.

Amelia gives Leonardo his MEDs and then retires for the day. The couple has an early night.

Eleven

Next morning, after his customary jog round the block, Albert wakes up Leonardo for his physiotherapy session. They breakfast together and then Albert leaves with his lunch prepared by Amelia, as usual.
Albert prefers carrying lunch from home even though the kitchen of the facility provides three meals. His schedule is tight and he prefers to walk around and check on the welfare of the facility rather than spend that extra time in the cafeteria.

His diligence towards his work and duty had enabled the facility to get ranked in one of the top ten correctional facilities. His co-workers are aware of it and this is their prime reason for not letting him go. Instead, they swore to find the traitor who was trying to push their progress down.

***

Leonardo meets his physical therapist, Beverly who is a tall lanky woman with an intense look. Amelia is a little taken aback by her attitude but thinks that perhaps it is her professional manner. Once the paperwork is done, she starts promptly and is very precise in her instructions. Listening to her instructions, Amelia feels she must have been in the military, but later on when she reads her biography, which is displayed near the front desk, she finds that she is wrong.

Her success rate with her patients is remarkable since she never gets attached to their personal stories and is very clear-cut in her instructions. Amelia also hears that she scolds her patient if he or she is slacking and does not do their exercises as instructed. She even drops her patient, if they do not listen to her after repeated suggestions. Amelia does not like that attitude and thinks of consulting Albert prior to changing her.

Leonardo's first therapy goes well. He understands the program and Beverly writes it down for him too. They are supposed to meet her the day after that. Leonardo is excited but also nervous and hopes to progress well. Amelia can sense his nervousness and tries to put him at ease while thinking to herself, "I don't like her attitude. I must speak to Albert and ask for another therapist the first thing tomorrow morning."

They reach home and Leonardo is exhausted by his exercises so he wants to take it easy. She helps him to his room and then starts lunch when she sees that her answering machine is flickering. She clicks the button. There are two messages for her.

"Hi Amelia, this is Amy here. I hope Leonardo is doing much better. (Pause) Listen Amelia, our knitting club was wondering about the status of the scarves that you took responsibility for? With winters coming, the shelters need to get a head count for them so that they can promise people accordingly. I hope you understand (with a low voice). So, please get back to me soon. Thanks. Bye Amelia."

Amy and Amelia were volunteers to a knitting club, which provided scarves to shelters.

Amelia is upset and a little furious with her friends for not understanding her situation. Then she realizes that life has to go on for others and if she has taken up a commitment to deliver the mufflers then she ought to deliver it by the date she had promised.

Amelia had taken the responsibility of completing four scarves in a month and she had only finished two. She was on her third scarf, which was just halfway done and the month end was approaching in another week's time.

Just then the second message starts to play.

The other message was from Maria who had come to know from Mateo about Leonardo's accident and wanted to offer her service with regards to any books that Amelia's son would like to check out from the library.

Hearing that, she was filled with gratitude and she takes a deep breath and thinks this through rationally.

She calls Amy and switches on the speakerphone so that she could talk while cooking.

"Hi Amy, this is Amelia here. I got your message. Yeah, Leonardo is doing much better and has started his physical therapy from today. I am hoping that he goes back to school in another week or so."

Her voice went a little low, "I have completed only two scarves, I am sorry. I can complete the third one by the month end and that's about it."

Amy offered to knit the fourth and that lifted up her spirits. "Thanks Amy. You are a gem. I will drop off the wool for the fourth scarf so that you could start knitting."

Amy offers to come by and meet up Leonardo and pick up the wool. Amelia asked her to come in the evening.

By the time she has finished the call; lunch is ready. She calls Leonardo but he is too tired to move. So she takes lunch to his room, ham sandwiches and some hot soup. Leonardo likes his sandwich with pickle so Amelia has put some in his plate.

While having lunch, Amelia updates Leonardo about her friend Amy and Maria. Leonardo appreciates the gesture. After lunch he returns to his books and Amelia gets out her knitting so that the incomplete scarf is done by month end.

Twelve

Javier has not cracked under interrogation, even though he is bleeding profusely. Mateo had volunteered to take charge of the interrogation, so that Albert is free of controversy. Albert is deeply grateful to Mateo for this.

Albert is sitting in his office worrying about this when Peggy pings him and informs him that the county sheriff, Mr. Dennis Laurelwood is on the phone. News about a guard being arrested and being questioned has spread like fire. He wants clarifications from Albert.

The warden was not very happy about the leak of news but keeps his voice steady and answers the questions. He suggests the sheriff to come by to their facility for an in-depth discussion regarding this since it is not appropriate to discuss this issue over the phone.

Laurelwood is slightly reluctant, but then agrees to come by early evening. Albert pages Peggy and asks her to keep that slot exclusive so that now there are no interruptions in that meeting. Then he starts to put together all the necessary paperwork that he needs to show the sheriff.

He even calls Mateo, John and Dr. Beringer for a quick meeting so that he can get the latest updates on Javier, and Ricardo. Sensing the anxiety in his voice they come over immediately. Mateo and John enter together and Robert arrives after a few minutes. They sit down and wait patiently for Albert to initiate the conversation.

"Please update me on anything latest on Ricardo or Javier, anything I may have missed out." Saying that he pulls out the log he maintains about these two convicts and their questioning.

Mateo has been giving exhaustive reports every day about the interrogation. Dr. Beringer's report about the wounds sustained and treatment administered is also entered in the logbook, so are John's comments as he supervised the whole affair. Once satisfied that he has not missed any vital information, he thanks his co-workers and asks them to head their way.

Albert goes for a quick stroll before his meeting with the sheriff to clear his mind and get fresh air. This is his mantra for staying calm and focused prior to any crucial meeting.

He returns to his office just in time for Peggy to announce the arrival of the Sheriff. Albert straightens his uniform, places his folder in front of him and stands up to greet the visitor. Sheriff Dennis Laurelwood is as tall as Albert with broad shoulders and good physique and has a thick luxuriant mustache, which played a major role in his personality. He was aware of it.

Albert shakes his hand and gestures him to be seated. The Sheriff makes himself comfortable by removing his hat and unbuttoning his jacket buttons.

"So, Albert what is it that I hear? A guard has been stripped from his duties, put in a cell and is being subjected to torture. Please explain this, my friend."

He sits back and plays with his mustache, letting the word 'friend' sink in. He did not want to antagonize Albert. His habit of playing with his mustache normally distracted people but Albert is used to him, and so does not pay much attention to it.

Albert starts his narration and shows him proofs like the resignation letter of Peter, the drug exchanged between convict 457 and Ricardo. He mentions the motive of Javier and Ricardo behind the drug, and also tells him that the name behind the operation has not yet been unfolded.

The sheriff listens to the warden attentively and then says. "This does not look good, Albert."

Albert nods while tapping his fingers on the desk.

"We have to get to the bottom of it before anybody gets hurt. The prime culprit is out there and can strike anytime." Dennis says with concern.

Albert updates him about how the facility has been double guarded and hiring has been frozen.

Sheriff suggests, "Albert, let's keep a watch on the families of the two captives. Where do they go? Whom do they connect with? I can put my people on this, and let's hope for the best. Keep me in the loop if anything new develops."

Albert nods and gives him the addresses of Javier and Ricardo's families. Laurelwood takes the paper, wears his hat and heads out after shaking hands with Albert. He returns unexpectedly when Albert is busy organizing his folder. Albert looks up and is surprised to see him again "Oh by the way Albert I forgot to commend you on your way of handling this case. Well done, my friend." He patted Albert's shoulder, and Albert stood up and shook hands with him.

After the sheriff's departure a much happier and confident Albert calls on his three trusted deputies and updates them on the latest development.

Thirteen

Amelia knits until her hands tire and then takes a nap, waking up to the sound of the doorbell. Amy has arrived as promised. She greets her warmly and asks her to come in. Leonardo is still working at his desk. He looks up as she enters his room.

Amy Hunt is a stout fun loving lady in her sixties. Her son, Sheldon had graduated and was settled in Los-Angeles. Her husband owns a plumbing business.

She has brought a small box of candy for the boy.

"Hello Leonardo. How are you doing?"

"I am good, Mrs. Hunt. Thanks for the candy and for your concern."

"Oh you are welcome son. Get well soon so that your mom can start mingling with us. We miss her already."

Amelia smiled gently, "Well thank you Amy. I am flattered."

Amy sat with Leonardo and discussed his academia and plans while Amelia went in the kitchen to get them something to drink

When she brought the cups in, Amy got up and put a cup for Leonardo on his desk, "Study well, sunny boy and get well soon."

She took a cup for herself and both ladies went out into the living room.

As they sat down, Amy looked at Amelia and commented, "You have lost weight. Is something troubling you?"

Amelia first avoided that question but after being coaxed, she confides in her friend. It is a great relief to her to give voice to her stress; her husband's job is on the line, her son is injured and once again dependent on her. Once all this is out, she feels so light as if someone just lifted a rock off her shoulders. She finds herself sitting up straight.

Amy sees this and pats her shoulder for added comfort. She adds, "You know, you could have just called me and talked your soul out. Just talking helps, Amelia."

Amelia smiles and nods, "I will from now onwards. Thanks Amy."

They finish their beverage, which was warm by now. Amelia shows her the completed scarves and gives her the wool for the fourth muffler. Amy offers her to knit her half completed scarf, but she refuses the offer and says, "I hope to come in person and hand it over by the end of the month."

Amy nods "Amen, to that."

They laugh and then Amy departs.

Amelia starts dinner preparation and her mind drifts to her husband's work and his work related problems. Stirring the pot and boiling rice does not require much concentration so she let her mind wander. Dinner is nearly done and she is about to set the table when Leonardo calls her, "Mom"

She places the dishes on the table and heads towards his room, "What's up, Leonardo?"

"I was thinking of doing my exercises. Could you please help me?"

"Sure son, I will be happy to help you." Even though her back is hurting since the morning, she does not allow a frown come on her face.

She helps him up and holds his leg when he asks her to. She is a good assistant. The exercises take thirty minutes and the doorbell interrupts them. Amelia excuses herself and gently helps him to the bed and goes to get the door. She is happy to greet her husband and hug him tight. He is her best stress buster. They come in and Leonardo shouts from his room, "Hey dad"

Albert responds, "How is it going, son?"

Amelia interrupts, "Honey, could you just help Leonardo finish his exercises, while I get your chilled beer."

"Sure, I think I can do that." He smiles, and goes in the room to help Leonardo finish off with his remaining stretches, impressed that Leonardo was taking his physiotherapy seriously.

Amelia hands the bottle to Albert and sits down to tell him about her doubts about the therapist, "Leonardo is doing good, but his therapist is very professional and I get cold vibes from her."

Albert looked at her with curiosity, "What do you mean? A therapist ought to be professional,"

"I mean, she does not smile or ask how he hurt himself. She does not express any sort of feelings." Leonardo can understand what his mom is trying to express and adds, "Dad, she is very strict and says that if I do not exercise twice a day, she will drop me as her patient and I will have to look for another therapist. This is not right, dad."

Albert puts the bottle to his mouth and gulps it down rapidly, and then reasons with his son.

"Leonardo, this is very good, my son. This way you will be exercising religiously and you will gain your strength back. Your success is her success." He says this with a smile.

Amelia interjects, "But honey, she could do all this with a smile as well. She looks so cold and remote, as if we had forced this onto her."

Leonardo agrees with his mom.

Albert feels like a minority here. He restates, "I feel you should stick to her because she means business. How about you take 3 more sessions with her and see your progress. Depending on how you feel then, you could drop her and go to another therapist. In fact, I have this feeling that she will make you better by then." He states this with confidence while taking a few more sips of his beer.

Mom and Leonardo nod and chime in, "Sounds reasonable."

Amelia and Leonardo laugh and hug. Then she speaks in exactly the same tone as Leonardo's therapist, Beverly and announces without a smile, "Dinner will be on the table in ten minutes. If you boys don't come out within that time, go feed yourself in a restaurant."

Leonardo's eyes widen and he looks at his dad, "Oh oh, dad we are in big trouble."

Albert says, "I should postpone my changing of clothes until later. Let me help you to the table and it should be NOW, son." He helps Leonardo get up slowly. While doing so, he sees the box of chocolates on his bedside. He inquires about them and Leonardo updates him about the visit of Amy.

Both the boys chuckle and start walking to the table slowly.

Amelia has finished placing dinner on the table and was about to sit when she saw them come looking anxious. She giggles and says solemnly "Atta boys, time is ticking, hurry up!"

Once the boys are settled in their chairs, she mellows down and serves them dinner.

Dinner done, kitchen settled, Leonardo goes back to his desk. The couple sits on the couch in their favorite position and updates each other about their day. Amelia mentions Amy's visit while Albert talks about the Sheriff visiting the facility and how he had a plan for the current incident. Both were glad that the day ended well. Albert turned on the television while Amelia started knitting. They shared a few words and comments on the show now and then. Albert starts yawning and goes in to change. He beckons Amelia to join him in the bedroom but she insists on knitting a bit more. By the time, Amelia comes in; Albert is asleep.

Fourteen

Days flow into weeks and Leonardo shows progress with his therapist, Beverly. On the last day of his therapy, Amelia and Leonardo are surprised to see her smile. They treasure the smile and have a lot to say about it to Albert.

Leonardo resumes school and is meeting his friends and Sophia on a regular basis. He values friendship even more after his accident and knows how to juggle time between friends and academia.

His fondness for Sophia is growing, and they have become close and would even exchange a peck or two.

Albert's facility is under constant vigil and Javier and Ricardo are still in isolation. They have still not got the name of the master planner. Mateo, John, and Albert often get impatient but pacify each other by saying, "Haste makes waste."

When weeks turn into months, the facility cannot afford to make their guards work overtime to keep up the constant surveillance. They need more manpower to achieve that. But with the constant cuts due to inflation that is not possible. So, Albert proposes having a key surveillance every alternate day, which later on becomes twice a week and then once a week.

Sheriff and Albert are in constant touch about this particular case and as the months pass by, they think that the master planner has abandoned this plan and has found some other motive.

They do not realize that this person is just biding his time, working cautiously and will strike when the iron was hot.

****

The senior year is coming to an end. For the prom night Leonardo invites Sophia. She has anticipated this night hundreds of times in her mind and her dress and accessories are ready. When asked, she tells him this and he is very impressed.

The night finally comes; Leonardo borrows his mom's car and goes to her home to pick her up. He goes inside and meets her parents. They are an Asian couple from Vietnam. Sophia is a US citizen since she was born here. Sophia's parents like Leonardo as they find that he is a polite young man and respects their daughter. They have met his parents in one of the school events and admired their principles. Being immigrants they have always been worried about their daughter's future, but are happy with her choice. They are aware that Sophia is serious about this boy and often wonder if he had the same type of feelings for her. They do not want Leonardo to break her heart.

When Leonardo comes to pick up Sophia for the prom night, she is still getting ready. Her dad asks him to be seated while he is watching television. He is a quiet man and does not talk much; her mom does most of the talking in their family. Sophia's mom thinks this to be an appropriate moment to ask him about his feelings and sits down next to him. Leonardo moves away a little to keep some distance between them. She smiles and comes to the point since they do not have much time before her daughter steps out of the room. "You must have seen how Sophia admires you."

Leonardo is confused where this was going and he nods and replied, "Sure, Mrs. Pham. I admire for all that she does for me." She hastily cuts his conversation while constantly glancing towards Sophia's room. "But, do you have the same feelings for her?"
Leonardo is embarrassed to be asked such a question. But he replies immediately," Mrs. Pham I have the same feelings for her and admire her." He went ahead explaining, "If you feel I will break her heart, don't even think about it. I am very serious about her."
Mrs. Pham is thrilled to hear that and she covers his hand with hers and squeezes it softly, "Thank you!"

She gets up and calls, "Sophia, what is going on? Leonardo has been waiting for you for over an hour."

Leonardo turns towards the television and her dad; Mr. Pham is still staring at the television set, with not a single care in the world.

Leonardo looks at the watch and then the TV set. Finally, he hears a sweet and familiar voice, "Hi Leonardo, sorry to keep you waiting."

Leonardo turns to her. She is looking ravishing. He had never seen her so beautiful. Her beautiful face has been enhanced with makeup, her lipstick emphasizes her perfect lips, her long eyelashes make her eyes look larger and her hair is perfectly curled. She is wearing a lovely dress. He says with admiration, "Sophia you look stunning, and you will outshine all the girls out there."
Sophia blushes and looks around hoping her parents have not heard this. She whispers in his ear, "You look sharp as well, Leonardo."

Leonardo looked down at his tux and whispers, "Thank you."

He hands her the prom corsage, which she wears on her wrist.

Her mother asks them to pose together so that she can take a picture of them as a couple. They blush initially but then strike their finest pose. After clicking a few pictures, Sophia takes the camera from her mom to take pictures at the prom.   They head for Leonardo's car after being reminded of the curfew time.

This is Leonardo's first party with his friends, and being unsure of how long he would stay, he did not pitch in with his friends in a limo.

They reach school and are greeted by their friends. Leonardo, being reserved by nature prefers to stand and watch others dance. Sophia makes sure he is at ease. They dance a bit, and then spend the evening in the sidelines.

Sophia loves the way he offers to get some punch for her so that she stays hydrated and kisses him on his cheek, and Leonardo likes that. They leave early, since Sophia senses Leonardo's boredom and whispers in his ear, "I am hungry, let's get out of here."

Leonardo is happy to hear the words. He immediately gets up like a charged bunny and when asked for a reason for their early departure, tells the others that Sophia wants to get a bite to eat then they might come back. Once in the car, he asks, "So, what do you feel like eating?"

"Nothing, I have had so much of punch that I am full."

Leonardo looks at her with curious eyes, "But you said you were hungry."
"Yup, I did, so that we could get away from there. I could sense that you want to head out."

He smiles and edges towards her in appreciation for her gesture. She brings her head all the way towards his chest. Leonardo drives to her home, and though

Sophia wishes he would drive to someplace else, she is too shy to tell him so. She is disappointed since she wants to hang out with him, but he does not get the picture. He has stuff on his mind, his assignments, some pending paperwork, and he keeps talking about it and she pretends to listen.

Finally when the car tires screech to a halt outside her home, she forces a smile and thanks Leonardo. She is about to get out, when Leonardo holds her hand, and pulls her towards him. Their lips meet for the first time and there was magic in the air.

There is no hesitation from either of them even though it is their first kiss; it was if they both had longed to do this for a long time.

They did not care how awkward it felt. Just being in each other's arms felt like heaven to them. Sophia breaks loose with a giggle and wishes him Goodnight. Leonardo waits until she goes in before he starts to drive to his place.

Sophia's mom, Hua is curious why she is home so early. It is only 10pm and two hours to her curfew. Sophia is in another world and does not care to answer her questions. Hua does not catch the excitement since she is happy to see her daughter content and home. She wishes her good night and goes into her room. Sophia cannot sleep the whole night as she relives the kiss again and again. It was her perfect moment and she was not ready to analyze it or go into the depth of it.

When Leonardo reaches home, his mom is knitting. She is also surprised to see him home so early, but the smile on his face said a lot about the evening. So she does not question him about his early arrival and let him be in the moment.

Leonardo goes to his room and tries hard to focus on his work. His mind is not co-operating, so he thinks of calling it a night hoping to work the next day.

Both teenagers have a sleepless night. None of them can sleep so Leonardo calls her cell at midnight and she answers on the first ring.

"Uh, were you sleeping?" asks Leonardo.

"No, I could not."

"Oh me too." Leonardo answers quickly.

"So, is that normal that people don't sleep after their first, you know?" asks a curious Leonardo.

"I guess so," replies Sophia. "I have never experienced it until now, so can't tell."

They start to laugh. Then talk about the prom and finally when they can hear each other yawn, they call it a night.

Fifteen

Amelia's knitting club is keeping many people warm. All the woolen things they knit are delivered to shelters every month. Their knitting club has enrolled new members so that more orders can be delivered. The women occasionally meet for coffee and mingle on a personal level.

Leonardo is enrolled at SFSU. He chooses this as it is near home and also because of Sophia. He is doing his pre-requisites from a community college, which will take him approximately a year and a half and then transfer them to his university and work towards his bachelor's in Computer Science. His parents are happy with his decision
Albert gifts him a second hand car when he passes the high school to Leonardo's joy. "This car will take you back and forth from your community college." He pauses and then continues, "You could even take your girl out sometimes in it." He winks after that.

Leonardo blushes and takes the keys, calling out to Amelia, "Would you like to go for a drive with me?"

Amelia is thrilled, "Sure son, give me a minute. I'd love to."

Albert teases her, "Go enjoy honey. Later on he will not even ask you."

Amelia says, "Not funny!" and pulls his nose.

Leonardo laughs.

After the ride, he drops her back and says, "Mom, I would like to give Sophia a ride. I will be back in an hour's time."

She replies with a smile, "Sure, go ahead."

Leonardo parks outside his girl friend's home and calls her and asks her to come outside. She steps out a little surprised. She hears a honk as looks towards the car and sees Leonardo. She waves at him and goes to the car. "Let's go for a drive, Sophia."

Sophia is also very excited, "Sure, let's do it."

She goes into the house, informs her mom and then they go for a spin around the town.

During the summer break; Leonardo's friends plan an out-of-town trip prior to resuming schools. Leonardo is in two minds. Amelia can sense it and makes him talk out his pros and cons. Finally the cons side won and he agrees to go. He wonders if Sophia will be able to join in too, as her parents were conservative. But then they trust their daughter's instincts and allow her to go with certain conditions. A pact of trust is signed between Sophia and her parents and she climbed on the bus to Monterey. It is an expensive trip so, teens pitched in for the trip. Sophia and Leonardo sit together for this 2-hour bus trip and when they reach the hotel, they check in different rooms. Steve is Leonardo's roommate and Katie is Sophia's roommate for the two-night stay in this city.

That evening they strolled along the downtown and then dispersed for dinner to restaurants of their choice and met up in the hotel to crash in their respective rooms.

The next morning after their breakfast of donuts, coffee, they split again. Some teens decide to jog on the harbor. Leonardo teams up with Sophia and other friends Daren, Katie, Vincent and Steve and plan to hike in the Andrew Molera State Park. Since it is a two to three hour hike, they inform their other friends that they would be back by late noon.
With sunscreens and caps on, these six teenagers set out for some adventure. Luckily they agreed on the same trail so, hiking together was fun enlivened by jokes and laughter. On the trail they see a couple with a dog on leash about four feet away from them who are busy arguing. The man holding the leash drops it and the dog approaches them and began to sniff and bark at them. This happens a couple of times and the teens got cautious since the dog is not friendly, and want to get past them.
While the teens are passing in the heat of the argument, the man drops the leash again, and the dog gets hold of Steve's trousers. Steve starts to panic and shouts, attracting attention. The dog gets more irritable, jumps and grabs Steve's hand in its mouth. The couple stops arguing and get defensive over their dog's action. Instead of pacifying their dog they blame the teens. While Daren, Vincent,

Katie and Sophia are arguing with the couple, Leonardo bends down and strokes the dog, whispering soothing words into his ear. The dog turns towards Leonardo and let Steve go. A very relieved Steve started to wave his arms up in the air out of exhilaration. Everyone is glad that it is a happy ending. Sophia is proud of the whole incident and on the way back to the hotel; she takes Leonardo aside and expresses her feelings for him. He is overjoyed and replies, "I love you too." Their lips meet again, but they break off soon as their friends spot them in action and start to tease them.

The teens reach their respective homes safe and with good memories. Leonardo and Sophia are now a couple. The next academic year Sophia becomes a senior while Leonardo enters a semester at a local community college. This college is about eight miles away from his home. The car made it easy to commute and sometimes on the way back if Sophia's schedule matches his, he picks her up from her school and they hang out together for some time.

Leonardo has also started working part time in a coffee shop. He needs this extra cash for gas and for his dates. His parents are proud of his sense of independence.

Months roll by into another year. Sophia gets her enrollment from SJSU and she wants to major in English Literature. She also plans to do her pre-requisites from the same community college as Leonardo, and then transfer it to her enrolled college. Leonardo and Sophia get to see each other more often and both are happy with how their life was turning out to be.

Sixteen

Albert is busy with his facility and also treasuring his logbook of ex-convicts. He is in touch with them and gets a phone call from them once in a while about their welfare.

One Friday evening when he is about to head home, Peggy pages him about a certain call. Albert takes the call, and hears a familiar voice but he cannot place the man. The caller introduces himself as Willy. "Oh Hi Willy. How have you been?"

Willy, an ex-convict spent over six months in Albert's facility for burglary. Unemployment had taken a toll on his mental stability. He wanted to support his family but had no job. One day, walking back from the employment center, he saw a random house whose garage door had been left open. There were a lot of groceries lying in the garage. He assumed that the owner had shopped from a wholesale market and kept his extra grocery in the garage. Seeing that extra food lying in the garage, he gave in to temptation to take some away for his hungry family. He looked around and when he saw no one to stop him, he grabbed whatever his hands could hold on to and started walking out. Just then, the owner walked into the garage and saw Willy fled with the food in his hands.

The owner started to shout loudly, "Help, help! His neighbors heard the shout and seeing the man running with food, some started to chase him and one of them dialed the emergency number for help. Willy was taken in custody. That did not bother him, what bothered him was that the food did not reach his hungry family. When he reached the police station, he was allowed to call his family and inform them about his reason of arrest. Unfortunately the family did not have enough money to bail him out. His case was studied and they realized that he was a victim of inflation but still what he did was wrong. He was sent to Albert's facility where convicts were trained in various professions such as weaving baskets, academic classrooms, automotive and ranch training, so that he could get employment once he is out of the facility.

Willy took the training in a positive stride and worked hard. Six months passed by and the day he was released, his family came to pick him up. Albert saw how emotional he got when he was hugging his wife and two adolescents.

Once Willy was out, he managed to find small jobs thanks to the different training he had received at the facility. Then he had started a small business of barbed wires, which was doing well thanks to the increase in crime rate.

Willy updates Albert on what he is doing and how his business has grown. Albert smiles as his heart swells up with pride. Willy invites the warden for a wedding, to which Albert replied, "Wow, that is fantastic, Willy. I will definitely come to your kid's wedding."

Albert notes the time and the venue and even though he is curious of the short notice, he promises to be there, and he hangs up. Peggy informs him that Willy had also invited John to his son's wedding.

He takes out his logbook and enters in Willy's progress. Albert calls John and tells him about Willy's call and they both feel proud of his progress. They plan to attend the wedding together the next day.

When he reaches home, he updates about his ex-convict to Amelia. She is happy and comments, "You are doing a fine job, honey. Look how many lives you have touched. I am so proud of you."

Albert feels encouraged.
Next morning, while Albert is getting ready, he tells Amelia about his plan to go to Willy's son's wedding. She finds the last minute invitation very strange, but being happy with his progress. She tells him to take a bouquet with him. He nods.

He first wants to go in his uniform to the wedding, but then thinks it may be an inappropriate dress and so takes a change of clothes with him, intending to change into them in the evening.

As usual, he leaves, carrying his change of clothes. Amelia gets ready to go for her knitting meet.

Albert and John meet at the scheduled time near the parking. John has not planned ahead and is still dressed in his uniform while Albert had changed into his casual clothes. Looking at Albert in his attire John remarks, "Oh, I wish I had thought this over. I could have brought my clothes as well. Oh bummer!"

They laughed and Albert started to drive. On their way, Albert picks up a bouquet. When they reach the church, the ceremony is on. They seat themselves. The ceremony reminds Albert of the day he married Amelia. They both were so young and Amelia was so fragile. The church they got married in was a historic one and they were on the waiting list for a month to get married there. This thought brings a smile to his face.

He also recalls how his parents were excited about the wedding and hired the best of caterers and music band. The memories of his marriage and the laughter he had shared with his new bride and his family seemed to take him years away from the present moment. He is brought back to the present when the priest at the church announced, "You may kiss the bride." There is loud jubilation and he starts to clap for the newly married couple.

The couple starts walking out of the church. John and Albert wait for all the family and friends to pass by. Willy sees them while hugging one of his family members and waves at Albert.

Albert waves back. Just then Albert notices a man who was looking at John with anger. He does not understand the reason for the bitter anger and wants to show him to John but the man disappeared in the crowd.

They are then ushered into the courtyard where lunch is being served. People start walking towards the courtyard when Albert sees the man again, who is walking towards John who is looking elsewhere. Then suddenly, the man takes out something from his pocket and aims it at John's chest. Albert lets go of the bouquet and screams John's name while pulling him out of the path of the attack. People start screaming and everyone turns towards them. Albert is supporting John who has fallen upon him and a knife is sticking in his shoulder, while he is groaning with pain.

Albert stares at the man and shouts, "Hold him, don't let him get away." But the people are looking at John and do not react, as they are still stunned. The person flees away.

Willy shouts, "Dial 911 and call an ambulance."

He comes towards Albert and helps John sit down. Albert, asks Willy to look after John while he runs after the person, but it is too late. The man sits in a car, which drives away. He is unable to note the number; he just notes the color and the make of the vehicle.

He calls the sheriff and informs him about the incident and sends an alert for a Silver Color Lexus heading towards the north of the city. By that time, the ambulance arrives and John is taken to the nearest hospital. Albert calls John's family and informs them, so that they can be by his side.

At the hospital, John is examined. He is lucky that his shoulder ligament is only bruised. He is bandaged and kept under observation for a day. John's wife arrives and has many questions for Albert, but the warden is busy calling for an artist and making many other phone calls.

When the artist arrives he sits down with him making a sketch. Once it is done, he shows the picture to John who says he has never seen that man before who stabbed his shoulder. Albert is getting angry at this bold attack on the officer.

As soon as he gets some information, he calls the sheriff immediately and updates him. Sheriff Laurelwood summons Willy to the station with his guest list, to compare the sketch with the people invited.

After Willy's son has left for his honeymoon, Willy goes to the station with the guest list. Albert is also there since he has one important question to ask Willy, this was a question everyone had on their minds, including Amelia and Peggy. Albert and sheriff Laurelwood greet Willy and while the sheriff was screening his guest list, Albert shows him the picture of the person who stabbed John. Willy has a frown on his face since he had never seen that person before.

Then Albert asks, "So, Willy how could you arrange a ceremony in a day's notice?"

Willy is serious and replies, "Exactly, we were also very surprised. We had our name registered for this church for a long time for our son's marriage. Then all of a sudden, a call came on Tuesday night telling us that there has been a cancellation for Thursday noon and we could have our ceremony. We were shocked and confused and not sure how we could manage everything in such a short notice. The person offered to help us and got everything done in our budget in 24 hours time. All we were asked to do was call our guests and come dressed up. We were overjoyed and felt blessed by this offer. Such opportunities hardly ever come by."

Sheriff and Albert look at each other and asked for the contact information of the person who had called. Willy looks at his call records and gives the details of the caller. Laurelwood calls the number and no one picks up the phone and there is no answering machine either. So he gets up and goes to investigate. Willy and Albert were left alone.

Willy inquires about John and Albert updates him while he fidgeting with his fingers. Just then Albert's cell phone rings. He sees Amelia's number flash on the screen, and tells Willy to be available whenever the Sheriff needs to see him or ask him questions. Willy gets up and leaves.

Albert answers the call, "Hi honey."

"Yes, the wedding was interesting." He replies to the question bitterly.

Amelia does not understand the tone, and the meaning of the word 'interesting' so she asks for clarification. He does not normally give out such information on the phone, but can't help himself. He tells her everything and then he is at ease. His fingers are not fidgeting anymore. He leaves for his facility.

Upon reaching the jail, he updates Peggy about the incident and asks her to send a memo to all the departments calling for a meeting, as it is better to tell the department heads personally than have them hear it from others.

The night at the Silva's is a somber one. When Amelia and Albert sit on the couch, they are very confused and worried. Although, Amelia tries to pacify Albert, she herself is worried and confused.

The sheriff is quick to capture the person who stabbed John within a few days of the incident. He is brought into his station for questioning. After numerous attempts of torture, he confesses that he hurt the wrong person. This was confusing again for the officers. Wrong person, then who is the target? The man does not answer this. Again the case is left hanging with no arrests made.

John resumes work. At times when he goes to Mateo he notices that Javier smirks at him. Initially, he could not understand it, but then started speculating that maybe Javier's case was connected to the suspect in the Sheriff's station.

He does not tell Albert as he is not fully convinced but keeps wondering if this is the case of mistaken identity. If Albert had also worn his uniform, he would have been the victim. And if John himself had been wearing casual clothes, none of this would have happened. His anxiety builds and he suffers many sleepless nights. He does not want to be a victim of mistaken identity again.

Seventeen

Months pass and another year too passes. Things are back to normal, even though the suspects are still in their respective lockups.

Albert is trying to keep a brave face amidst all this chaos. But emotionally he is a wreck. He wants to get to the bottom of these cases, but things are not moving to a conclusion. The sheriff has advised him to calm down since some cases take years to solve. But, since the Javier case revolved around him, he is nervous and hopes that no one else gets hurt.

This emotional conflict within him makes him neglect himself and he is not able to focus on his family or his health. He misses his annual checkups and even his ride to work; his car has been giving him problems lately. He is avoiding and postponing everything hoping to get back to other issues once this case is solved. Amelia watches him silently trying to pacify him every now and then, but things are not looking pleasant. The nights on the couch where the couple used to speak their hearts out to each other has stopped happening.

Albert is trying hard to be a good father and husband by not venting out his professional anger at home, but there are episodes when he spews his venom at Amelia and the scene becomes ugly and that leaves Amelia weeping.

Leonardo is now in his last quarter before transferring all his coursework to his university. He tries to stay focused and is grateful to his parents for all the support despite the daily tension in his dad's job. In his heart of heart, he despises that job and has always hoped that once he got his dream job, he will ask his dad to resign and lead a life without these unruly convicts.

Unfortunately, fate has something else stored for Leonardo.

On a cold rainy February evening, Albert's car stops midway while he is heading home. His car had been giving him problems for some time and he has neglected its maintenance. He gets out of the car and opens the hood and checks the machinery, which looked fine. Then he checks the oil by inserting the dipstick, which came out dry. He mutters to himself, "I should have taken care of this car, it needs maintenance."

He is completely drenched and the car would not start. He starts looking at the road where drivers are driving by slowly since visibility is poor. He places the dipstick on one side of this hood and starts to dial for road help. Just then a car stops behind his vehicle. He does not notice this until a stranger approaches him. He is wearing a raincoat and has a smile on his face.

"Hi there" the stranger says.

Albert replies back with courtesy.

"How have you been? It seems you've been neglecting your car and now it is giving you problems." He continues, "This is what happens when you put in all your energy in uplifting your convicts and try to help them. What did you get? Huh!" He shouts at him.

"Excuse me, do I know you?" Albert asks while trying to look carefully at the stranger whose head is covered with a hood. Visibility is near to zero because of the rain, and it is difficult for Albert to recognize this man. In the faint light from the headlights of the cars passing by, he can make out that the man was dark skinned, has a white beard and a few wrinkles around his eyes.

The man refuses to answer Albert's questions but continues to taunt him. Albert's confusion turns to anger. He turns away from this hooded man, and starts to dial for help. This annoys the man, "Hey you, I am talking to you. How dare you turn away!" and he pushes him towards the road.

Albert tries to balance, but his phone falls on the road. He tries to be polite, "Listen, I don't know you. Either introduce yourself or please go away. I can call for help."

The man starts shouting at him and pushing him. Incensed, Albert retaliates by pushing him back.

This angers the man who pushes him harder and Albert fell on the road. He hears a loud honk and sees headlights approaching and comes to his feet immediately to avoid getting crushed by the approaching car.

The stranger starts laughing and brandishing the oil dipstick.

"What are you doing?" asks Albert.

The man just laughs and says, "I don't like you. I don't like the way you change the convict's lives. Such people got to go."

This threat brings adrenaline into Albert's system and he shouts back, "Oh so you are the person who has been after me? What is it for you to not like? The community is becoming a better place to live in. What is it in for you?"

The man hits him on the shoulder with the dipstick, "My business is getting affected. The reformed convicts are of no use to me. They want to live a good life and it has affected my drug business. I want my profits back. I want back MY life." He shouts hard into his ear.

"I gave you many signals to change, but you did not. You have to go so that I can get back my lifestyle and my profits back." He kept hitting him repeatedly.

Albert falls down again, this time near his phone. He quickly picks it up and pressed TALK. The emergency number was already dialed, and he could hear a lady speak, but he could not reply. He slips the phone in his pocket while getting up hoping that the lady on the phone hears this conversation and sends help.

The man in the raincoat does not see the phone and continues attacking him. Albert tries to defend himself but is getting hit most of the times.

Albert's shoulder and back are in pain due to the constant blows and he has sustained bruises on his head. He keeps trying to get up and hit back to get control over the fight, but is unable to. He hopes that the lady has dispatched help while trying to defend himself from this crazy man.

This hooded man pulls out a white substance from his pocket and then forces it into Albert's mouth and hits him again. Drenched and bleeding, Albert tries his best to protect himself but the last few months have taken a toll on his body and his emotions. The substance forced into his mouth is very intoxicating, and, whenever he spits it out, the man forces some more into his mouth.

He finally gives up and lies unmoving, in the puddle, covered with wet dirt, his mouth stuffed with that white substance he was forcibly made to swallow. Help arrives, and the culprit hears the siren. He quickly drops the oil dipstick and gets into his car and drives away.

The cops arrive on the scene and page an ambulance, which takes ten minutes to arrive. In the meantime, they examine Albert and see his identity

card. They ring up the Sheriff and update him about the accident. The Sheriff asks them to take him to a nearby Emergency
Albert has stopped moving by then.

The paramedics examine Albert and transfer him to the ER.
Albert's body arrived in the ER where the Sheriff has also reached. Unfortunately, he is pronounced dead.

Laurelwood searches in Albert's records and finds his home number and calls it.

He hears Amelia's soft voice and gives her the news. She is devastated and shrieks as she hangs up the phone.

Leonardo hears her shriek and comes into the living room, asking what happened. She tells him and he is shocked and keeps staring at her. Then he helps her up and says, "Let's go to the hospital, mom."

Amelia can hardly walk; she is still shocked by the news and very upset with her fate. She keeps thinking, "What wrong did we do? We always compromised with destiny and did not lament about our future and still she took him away."

Leonardo is furious too. He did not expect his dad to go away like this. His dad gave so much to the facility and in return he got pain and suffering and this kind of ending. He has tears in his eyes while driving, but controls his emotions since he wants to be strong for his mom.

They reach the hospital and the cops directed them to a room where Albert's body is placed. He is cleaned up and covered with a clean white sheet. He has a peaceful expression on his face as if wanting to sleep for a long time.

A doctor is standing next to his bedside.

Amelia has not seen this peaceful expression on Albert's face for a long time and just keeps staring at him, hoping that he is actually sleeping and turns towards Leonardo, "Shh, he is sleeping. Let us sit here until he wakes up." Leonardo presses her shoulder, "Come on Mom." He leads her to Albert's body.

Leonardo touches his dad's forehead and plays with his hair, just as he did when he was alive. He cannot control his tears and Amelia sees the tears fall on Albert's cheek. She looks at her son, and then starts to cry loudly uncontrollably.

Leonardo hugs her tightly and cannot control himself anymore.

The doctor wants to update them on how Albert passed away, but the son and the mother are still absorbing the fact that he had died and the thought of the cause of death had not come up yet.

The sheriff who was standing outside, comes to Albert's bedside, and introduces himself. Amelia nodded since she had heard about him from her husband.

"I am very sorry for your loss, Mrs. Silva. We will get to the bottom of this, I promise." He said.

Leonardo interjects furiously, "What have you been doing for the past one year? My dad was going crazy about these unsolved cases and he was emotionally stressed. Now he is no more with us."

"We don't care if you get that person or not. He has done his job and must be opening a champagne bottle someplace, while we cry over our loss." He adds.

Amelia tries to console Leonardo by putting her hand on his chest, but he can't be controlled. He is spitting venom and Amelia realizes how upset he was with the tension at home due to the arguments his parents had over Albert's professional life.

She let him talk while keeping her head down and taking deep breaths. She tries to come to terms with the present situation by thinking of Albert as one character of her life, who is no more, but unfortunately the drama of her life has to go on, and so she has to pick up the pieces and start walking at least for the sake of her son.

She starts thinking about their savings and also her job prospects.

Just then she felt some light shining on her face and she spots a person with a camera and the other with a microphone coming towards her. It takes her a moment to understand who they were and then she tells the sheriff, "No reporters, please."

Sheriff respects her choice and tries to shoo them away. The reporters did not care for his command. Finally the cops push them outside.

The Silva's led a simple life and they do not know the importance of Albert's position until his death. Although the governor had awarded Albert for his remarkable services to the facility and for bringing positive changes in the conduct of the convicts, Albert always thought that it was his job and the commendation did not affect his mind. He was a warden of a reputed facility. The wardens of other jails would consult him for different programs, and he was always helpful to them. In fact, Peggy, his secretary would joke with him to start a consulting firm as a side business. He had actually started making plans of doing it once he retired from his existing job. Little did he realize that he would lose his life while fighting for what he was applauded for?

Leonardo and Amelia sit in one corner of the room sobbing and trying to come to terms with their loss, while the Sheriff makes arrangements for the funeral.

It is soon all over the media that the warden was killed. John, Mateo, the guard and Dr. Beringer rush to the hospital. They are deeply shocked and feel like they had lost a family member but put a brave face in front of Albert's family and try to pacify them.

Leonardo's friends come to know about it and come rushing to the hospital along with Sophia. She hugs him tight and he breaks into loud tears. Sophia is by Amelia's side throughout the ceremony. She ensures that the reporters do not bother her.

Wives of many guards and department heads are present to bid their final farewell to this high-ranking man. They are there for Amelia who has always been a part of important events in their lives and pitched in with goodies to make any occasion complete.

Since the ceremony is conducted late at night, most of the people attended and it is also being televised LIVE. All the officers of the facility are there, expressing their gratitude for this noble man. The county where the facility is located is flying their flag at half-mast to show their respect for this humble man.

Amelia and Leonardo reach their home early morning too tired to talk or cry anymore. They both settle on the couch and in no time, have slept off.

They are woken up by a phone call. Leonardo gets up and takes it. It is his grand dad from Portugal. News has spread fast especially since media are involved. When Amelia hears her dad's voice, she breaks down again and is unable to speak at all. Leonardo is by her side trying to console her.

Her parents are asking her to sell everything and come back. Amelia is a wise woman; she does not commit to anything and says that she will think about it.

Leonardo is relieved and thanks her for the decision she made by getting her a glass of water.
Amelia hugs him tight and says, "Sure, I have to make your career, son. Your dad would have wanted me to do that as well."

There is a ring at the door and her friend Amy arrives along with her knitting buddies. Amy has bought a pot of coffee and breakfast. She hugs Amelia tight and expresses her condolence and so do the other ladies.

Amelia cries but then controls herself. She asks Amy if she knows of anybody who would need knitting services. She wants to resume work.

Amy and her knitting buddies say that they will look around the let her know. Amelia requests them to treat this as important since she needs to keep the house running.

Leonardo hears all this and put his hand over her shoulder whispering into her ear, "Relax mom, we will get the money to run the house. You don't need to worry about it or think about working." Amelia looks at him with curious eyes but does not respond as she has company.

Amy gets up and serves breakfast to Leonardo and gives Amelia a cup of hot coffee. Her knitting buddies gradually leave, while she forces them to eat and after a while she also leaves too, after promising to come back again.

Leonardo and Amelia are now alone again.

Amelia brings up the topic of their present financial situation. "Leonardo, I have to work because we don't have enough savings to run the house and pay up our mortgage, son."

Leonardo comes and sits down next to her, "Sure, mom. I understand. I will take care of it. You don't need to take care of the whole burden. I am here to help out."

Amelia interrupts, "Son you have a goal to attain. Why don't you focus on that? In another two years you will get a good job and then I will sit back and relax." She tries to smile but with tears in her eyes.

Leonardo knows that his mom would not listen to his plan so, until it materializes, he lets it be.

"Okay, mom you find a job and I will also look for one. Then let's discuss the strategy."

Amelia is still a little confused but keeps quiet.

In the evening, Leonardo's friends from school come over. They were a big group. In fact, there was not enough space to seat them. But they did not bother; some stood, some sat on the floor while some stood outside the house waiting for their turn to express their condolence to Leonardo and his mother.

Amelia looks at the teens and then at Leonardo, grateful for the accident that made Leonardo pause and find friends. If that had not happened, he would have been devastated today with the loss of his dad, and lonely without a shoulder to cry on. Today, he is being a strong son for his mother but having a support system to express his insecurities is essential for his emotional growth.

She observes how Leonardo reacts at seeing so many teens come to express their condolence and at that moment, he reminds him of her husband, who was also very approachable and humble. Sadly, he did not get his way in this world and she shed a tear over it.

She hopes and prays that Leonardo gets solace in whatever career path he chooses in life. She crosses her fingers as a gesture to ask the Almighty for direction.

Sophia is being a great help in their home. She makes sure that all his friends meet Leonardo to express their feelings. Once everyone left, she arranges things back to how they were. Sophia's parents come in with dinner and her mom Hua ensures that Amelia eats. Amelia is having a hard time ingesting food as it reminded her of how much her husband liked the food. Sophia's dad, Vincent sits quietly besides Leonardo who is also trying hard to focus on eating for dinner has always been their favorite meal of the day. He chokes on that memory and goes to get a bottle of water from the refrigerator and sees bottles of beer. This again reminds him of his dad, and he gets teary eyed. He shut the fridge and leans against it, he so badly wants this to be a dream since; he is feeling so helpless and does not know how to be strong for his mom and also run the house.

He whispers a silent plea to his dad's soul. "Dad, I wish you had not left us. We will miss you dearly. Dad, give me the strength to look after mom. Give me ideas on what to do, how to do. I am clueless right now, dad. Please help me."

Just then a hand rests on his shoulder.

He quickly opens his eyes and sees Sophia.

"What are you doing here, Leonardo? Come and eat your food."

Leonardo nods, "Sure. Just came in to get some water."

The Phams clean the dishes, table and leave. Sophia hugs Amelia and Leonardo and promises to be there the next day.

Leonardo is grateful. He needs her support.

Amelia goes and sits on the couch, reminiscing about all those years with Albert by her side, her head on his shoulder, as they would exchange their day's happenings. She so longed for it to come back. She joined her hands and brought them to her forehead in desperation asking for another chance.

Leonardo stands near the couch and watching all this, not knowing how to react to all this since he is also in an emotional turmoil. She tries to come to terms with the fact that when time has passed, it would not come back. Then she unfolded her hands, wipes her tears and goes for a shower.

Leonardo sits on the couch and stares blankly at the television. He does not know what to do. His body is tired but he cannot sleep.

His mom comes out in her nightdress, sees Leonardo on the couch and sits down next to him and forces a smile. She puts her hand on his arm and says with a deep breath, "Thank god we have each other." Leonardo's eyes fill with tears, which he quickly wipes and hugs her, "Sure, mom. I will always be there for you."

They sit like that for a long time until their eyes start to close. Leonardo helps his mom to her bedroom and tucks her in. She laughs slightly and comments, "Times change so quickly, son. There was a time, I used to tuck you in and now you are doing that to me." Leonardo has tears in his eyes as he leaves her bedroom.

Amelia is very tired and as soon as her head hits the pillow, she falls asleep.

Eighteen

Leonardo switches off her bedroom light and goes into the hall. On the side table is his dad's picture in his uniform and being commemorated by the governor. He picks it up and looks at it reminded of the function. They had been so proud of him and his achievements. Leonardo admired what his dad did, changing the lives of many by giving them a path to walk on. He gave a positive direction to people who were unfortunate. He was the illuminator in their lives, and their families today led a decent and a respectable life, thanks to his father.

It was a hard and difficult task, but he had been adamant to do it. The appreciation speech given by the governor was still loud and clear in his ears. He felt very proud of his dad then and even now, while he is holding his picture. His dad did things that were tough and made them doable. This inspired him to think of taking up a part time job in the same facility as his dad, since he wanted to be near him and hopes that his father will guide him through this journey of life.

He places the frame back and happy that he has got some direction, goes to his room and crashes on his bed.

Amelia wakes up early next morning and she takes a while to come to terms on what happened the previous day and then wiping her tears, she goes into the kitchen to brew some coffee. Out of habit, she starts to get lunch for Albert then realizes the truth and goes and sits on the couch staring helplessly around the room.

Leonardo wakes up to the noise in the kitchen and comes into the hall. He takes a while to absorb the loss and then goes and hugs his mom. After a few minutes he goes to the kitchen, and gets two cups of coffee.

They sit quietly together and sip it.

Then Leonardo tells her, "Mom, I plan on taking a part time job in dad's facility."

Amelia turns to him with a frown, "I don't understand you. What is inspiring you to go back to the place, which was the reason of your dad's death? Forget that place." She says sternly coffee.

Leonardo gets up and picks up a frame containing his dad's picture and brings it to her. "Look at this picture, mom. We were all so proud of that day when the governor honored dad. Remember the speech he made for my dad. Remember, how we all were so proud of him."

Amelia takes the frame and sheds a few tears and nods, "Yes that was such a memorable moment in our lives." She wiped her tears and continued, "But, what if the person comes to harm you as well, I have no other soul to depend on, my son."

Leonardo sat next to her and replied, "Mom, I am not becoming a warden. I will just do a part time job there and continue with my studies. My goal is someplace else."

Mom nods, and gets up, saying, "We can leave together to the facility after their breakfast, your Dad used to say ..."

Leonardo chimes in, "Breakfast is an important meal of the day." Both share the laughter.

Leonardo has a quick shower while Amelia prepares breakfast. They sit down to eat together. The chair that Albert used to sit on is empty. They stare at the chair and look down with a heavy heart then, Leonardo brings up his glass of orange juice and says, "Cheers, dad" Amelia looks up instantly and stares at the chair as if Albert is there and then realizes that soul never dies, so picks up her glass as well and adds, "Cheers, Albert"

They finish their breakfast. Amelia goes for a shower while Leonardo cleans up the table and kitchen.

He hears the telephone ring and answers it, "Hi, Sophia."

Leonardo updates her about her plans and his reasons for taking up the part time job. Sophia agrees with him and wishes him luck. They hang up promising to meet each other in the evening.

When Amelia hears the phone ring, her heart skips a beat, thinking it to be Albert calling for her. With a pang she realizes the reality and continues to get ready.

Amelia dresses up and reaches out for her perfume but then says to herself, "Who is it for?" She looked at her jewelry and skips that as well. Combing her hair she comes into the hall. She looks so plain without her jewelry. Leonardo is used to smelling her fragrance and turns to look at her in surprise. Then he takes her by the arm and leads her into her room asking her to put her regular stuff. She looks away from her dressing table and then Leonardo says, "Mom, you ought to live for me. I need a parent in my life." She is in tears but hearing that, she hugs him tight, sprays her usual fragrance and wears her trinkets and joins him.

She suggests, "I think I should call Peggy and check if they have appointed some head for his dad's position."

Leonardo agrees.

When Amelia starts to dial the number, she got into her usual habit and as Peggy picked up, she said, "Hi Peggy. Could you please transfer me to Albert?"

There is a shocked silence from the other end and then Amelia realizes the words she has uttered.

Leonardo comes and put his hand on her shoulder. She corrects herself, "I am sorry, Peggy. Ugh so, how is everything out there."

"It's going okay, Mrs. Silva. John Kemp has been appointed as the temporary warden for now, so that things continue to stay under control."

"Sure, I understand, Peggy." Amelia says.

"Could you please connect me to John? Leonardo and I wanted to come to meet him."

"Sure, Mrs. Silva. By the way, I cleared out Mr. Silva's desk and you could also take his box with you."

Amelia sighs, and reminds herself that life has to go on. She replies, "Sure, thanks Peggy."

John picks up the extension and speaks with courtesy, "Hello Mrs. Silva. How have you been?"

She pauses for a bit and replies, "I am okay, John." Then she continues, "Leonardo and I would like to come by to meet you. Will you be around?"

"Sure, I will be here."

She hangs up and brings her hands to her face and murmurs in embarrassment, "I have to be watchful of my actions. They have to change like everything has." Leonardo consoles her, "Mom, time needs to be patient in order for things to change. It is okay if you make such errors."

Amelia grabs her purse and they leave.

In the car, Amelia recalls the time when Leonardo offered to give her a drive when he got the keys to his car. She smiles silently and buckles herself up.

Nineteen

When they enter the facility, the guard salutes while opening the gates. They acknowledge it and drive in, parking in the garage. There they saw the parking space, which had Warden, Albert Silva's name. Leonardo parks next to it.

After parking their car, the mother and son stand in the parking space where Albert used to park daily. Amelia closes her eyes so that she could feel his vibes around her. Leonardo watches her and let her be in the moment. When she opens her eyes, she had a smile on her face and they start to walk towards the office.

The way is so familiar to them.

When they reach the office, Amelia pauses a bit before knocking on the door. Leonardo waits patiently for her to recover.

After knocking, they hear the voice, "Come in"

Leonardo pushes the door open and John immediately gets up and comes forward to greet them. Amelia nods and Leonardo shakes his hand.

They are directed to the chairs. Amelia is about to sit when she notices a big brown box sitting on one side of the room. She stares at it and John says, "That box contains Albert's things."

Leonardo replies, "Yes, thank you. We were updated about it by Peggy; will take it on our way back."

The three of them sit and Amelia glances around the room, fidgeting with her fingers. She recollects all those times with Albert in this office. Leonardo and John let her settle down before they start a conversation.

Amelia notices the silence and sees John and Leonardo waiting for her patiently. She smiles and asks, "How have you been John? Hope your arm is doing much better."

John looks at his arm, smiles and replies, "Thanks to Albert that I am here. He saved me. But, thanks for asking Mrs. Silva, I am doing much better." He continues, "We have a couple of candidates lined up for the warden position. I am just filling in until the county finds him."

He pulls out a file from his desk and places it on the desk. While pushing it towards Amelia he says, "This file contains the details on how Albert was killed. You did not want to hear about it in the hospital so, thought I forward this file to you." He continued, "Albert's finances such as his 401 (k) etc. will be discussed by the county's department. They will be contacting you in a week's time. They are working on it."

Amelia looks away from the file.

Leonardo pulls it towards himself and says, "Thank you Mr. Kemp. I will read it at my leisure."

Leonardo comes to the point, "Mr. Kemp I am looking for a part time job so that we can continue to meet the demands of our mortgage etc. So, is there anything that would be suitable for me looking at my qualifications?"

John informs them that there were many openings for a part time guard and asks Leonardo if he would be interested. Leonardo nods and John pages Mateo to come by.

They wait for a few minutes when there was a knock on the door. Mateo comes in, expresses his condolences again to the widow of the warden and his son. Amelia inquires about his son and his wife.

After the courtesies, John informs Mateo about Leonardo's desire to take a part time job as a guard. Mateo assured Leonardo, "I will be happy to train you for this and be there for you."

Mateo remembers their baby shower and how Mrs. Silva had taken interest in planning it out for his family. He feels indebted to them for this gesture and is glad to pay it back by helping Leonardo

Leonardo was pleased to hear Mateo's words and gets up and shakes Mateo's hand and thanks him.

Amelia thanks him, as well.

Mateo asks Leonardo to come to his office so that they can fill the necessary paperwork.

Amelia gets up and tells Leonardo, "Please go ahead with Mateo. I will wait for you in the car." Leonardo hands her the car keys.

John pages a guard to help pick up the brown box containing Albert's things and help carry it to the car. Amelia thanks John and heads towards the car, with the guard following her with the box.

Mateo and Leonardo went their way.

Peggy meets Amelia while she is walking towards the garage and exchanges a few pleasantries. Many people from various departments, who could not meet Amelia in person at the burial ceremony, left their work to pay their respects and say a few kind words about their deceased warden.

Amelia is overwhelmed with all the kind words, and wonders if they were spoken while Albert was alive. Usually a man becomes more important and valued when he is gone. The ordinary daily life tends to make everything for granted and mundane. She finds the journey to her car a very emotional and long one. Finally when she reaches it, she unlocks it and asks the guard to place the box in the back seat of the car. She thanks him and then goes and stands in the parking space that once belonged to her husband.

She stands there and her mind wanders into the past. She recollects her first trip to his office and her surprise at seeing the facility, she recollects on how pampered her son used to be whenever he visited his dad's office. The respect and admiration the office people gave her family was commendable and today they are giving Leonardo a part time job. Her heart is filled with gratitude and cannot ask for more. She thanks her husband in her heart and wishes that his soul rested in peace.

She goes and sits in the car and looks at the brown box sitting on the back seat. She looked around and since Leonardo is nowhere to be seen, she thinks of opening it and going through the contents of the box until he comes back.

She goes and sits next to the box and opens it. Each of the contents was wrapped individually with paper. This brings a smile to Amelia's face. She thanks Peggy in her heart for doing this.

Albert was a sentimental man. He had things saved from his childhood days, which he had got with him from Portugal when he immigrated like a stone carved in the form of a penny of Portugal currency. One of the workers had given it to him when he used to visit his dad's office as a kid. He had so many handcrafted knickknacks that Leonardo had made and gifted him on Father's day. All these had been treasured and were in good state. Amidst all that she saw the file. It was a file, which Albert treasured the most. It was his purpose in life. She opened it and saw the various names of convicts and their current situation. She is awed as she goes through the pages, with the names and details about the convicts' current job and location.

She wonders if the new warden would do the same but realizes that comparison will not lead her anywhere so stops that train of thought.

She is so busy browsing through that file that she does not hear her son come to the car until he taps on her windowpane. She looks up and smiles at him. She puts the stuff back in the brown box and comes forward to the passenger seat. Leonardo has a file in his hand. He sits behind the wheel and hands her the file.

She starts to look through the file and comments, "It looks like you are all set?"

"Yes, mom, I will start from tomorrow." He replies as he reverses his car.

Amelia nods and asks him how he will manage his studies.

 "Mom, I plan on finishing this quarter and then transfer all my pre-requisites to the university. I intend to take a semester break in college and then resume my studies there. I have taken the evening shift as a guard. I will go to the community college in the day and come here for my evening shift."

Amelia is concerned, "Son, it will be tiring for you. When do you plan on studying and doing your assignments?"

"I will manage mom," he replies with a smile.

Amelia pats his thigh and looks through the window, taking a few deep breaths and prays that he gets his goal in life.

They stopped at a local restaurant for a quick bite and eat quietly. Then they drive home. A stranger in a uniform, which read as 'Ken's Repair Service,' was waiting for them. Confused, they parked their car and approached him.

"Hello Sir" He greeted Leonardo.

Leonardo went and shook hands with him and greeted him back.

The man said, "These are the car keys and I could not find a parking spot nearby. Your car is parked diagonally."

Leonardo looked at the key chain and recognized the car, his heart thumped rapidly and he glanced at his mom. Amelia was standing behind him; she peeped over Leonardo's shoulder to see what he was holding in his hand and saw the keychain. She covered her mouth with her hand to avoid screaming.

The person offers to get the car near their home, but Leonardo refuses saying "No, I will get it."

The man turns to leave and then abruptly turns, informing Leonardo, "Oh, the repair has been paid so, no worries about it."

Leonardo nods, raises his hand as if bidding him bye.

He then turns to his mom and shows her the keys. Her hand is still covering her mouth, but she gathers courage by then and waves him to go get the car.

Leonardo nods, gets the car, and parks it in the driveway.

Amelia walks to the car and places her hand over the bonnet of the car and closes her eyes. She envisions all memories, good and bad, that she shared with her late husband. Leonardo is watching her from a distance. He does not want her to feel the pain but realizes that she needs closure, so he lets her do it.

In no time, Amelia is sobbing uncontrollably. She has a vision on how her husband was tortured and killed. Her face is red and she wants to shout out to the cruel world but there is nobody there to listen to her, and it will only disturb her son. So, she controls herself.

Leonardo comes and hugs her. They lock their cars and went inside.

Amelia goes to her room to freshen up while Leonardo sits on the couch with his head on the pillows, next to his dad's picture. He feels as if Albert was comforting him by stroking his head.

The doorbell rings and he is reluctant. But, realizing that his mom will have to get it, he drags himself to the door.

He opens the door. It is Sophia. They hug each other and Sophia walks in. She asks about his dad's car and he updates her about getting fixed. They sit together on the couch where he updates her about his taking a part time job as a guard. She skips a heartbeat. Sensing that, he hugs her and continues, "This is another way for me to be near my dad's job and I am sure he will guide me. This is important for me." He kisses her cheek and she blushes and wishes him good luck.

Amelia walks into the hall and Sophia gets up from the couch and greets her.
Amelia is pleased to see her and gestures her to be seated, while she goes into the kitchen to make some dinner.

The doorbell rings again. Leonardo answers it. It is one of his classmates who have come by to offer him his notes and update him about the missed classes.

Leonardo sits with him and listens attentively while he briefs him. Sophia goes to the kitchen to help Amelia.

Dinner is ready in no time. Amelia does not cook an elaborate meal, as Albert was the only one keen to have a good meal and with him not around, she does not bother much.

Once Leonardo's friends left, mother and son dined quietly. Leonardo feels uncomfortable with the silence and so he turns on the television.

He helps his mom clean up and goes in to work on his assignments.

Amelia sits on the couch and recalls her days with Albert as she helplessly stares at the television. There is a show going on, but she stares at it blankly while her mind is elsewhere.

Amelia dozes off with the TV set on. Leonardo is checking on her from time to time, and when he sees that her head was resting on the couch, he feels sorry for her. She is a lonely soul and needs something to keep herself occupied. He checks the watch and sees that it was only nine pm. So, he rings up Amy, her knitting buddy.

Twenty

Amy promptly answers it, "Hi Amelia. Good to hear from you. How have you been, dear?"

Leonardo says, "Hello Mrs. Hunt. This is Leonardo here."

She corrects herself, "Oh, hi Leonardo."

Leonardo comes to the point, "Mrs. Hunt I have a favor to ask of you. I plan on going back to college during the day. Mom will be alone. Could you come and give her company?"

"Sure Leonardo. That is not a problem. In fact, I wanted to speak to her about a paid proposition, which she can do from her home. So, it will be a good opportunity for me to brief her about it. I should be there by 10am"

Leonardo thanks her and hangs up.

He goes to his mom, wakes her up and helps her to her room and into bed. He tucks her in and switches off the light.

On his way to his room he switches off the television and goes back to studying.

Next morning, he gets up early to have coffee with his mom, and tells her that Amy will visit her, and then he gets ready for college.

Amelia is pleased to have a visitor and is looking forward to 10am. She makes breakfast and also a sandwich for Leonardo and put it a brown bag. Then they both had breakfast together while discussing their day and their plans.

Leonardo collects his books, his brown bag and after kissing his mom on the forehead and goes out and pauses as he sees his dad's car parked in the driveway.

He goes in and tells his mother, "Mom, I plan on taking dad's car to college and then to the facility."

Amelia is cleaning up in the kitchen. She turns back immediately and said, "No"

She then realized that she was being very abrupt and clarifies, "Listen son, I don't think we should meddle with that car. She is old now and needs to retire. I was actually thinking of selling her."

Leonardo looks at his watch and then said, "Mom, we should have this discussion later. But, I want his car today since I need him to guide me. It will be my first day where I will be out in this wild world without him and I need that car." He goes towards the drawer that holds car keys and exchanges his key to his dad's car and waves her goodbye.

Amelia does not reply, but she comes out and waves at him with a pensive smile. She stands there watching the car, as all those memories of her husband's demise come flashing back to her. She closes her eyes and says a short prayer for his soul and hopes that the car is not a witness to such horrifying incident again.

Amelia is a spiritual and intuitive person who has no planned agenda or goal for herself. Her family means everything to her and their happiness is her way to bliss and ecstasy. She is not dependent on them since she is an educated lady and can earn a living for herself but when she made a choice to marry and then have a baby; she decided to invest totally towards their well being and development.

She is aware that she was not a super woman. She does not try to control them, but makes efforts from her side to care and nurture for them, and leaves the remaining to destiny and their karmas.

She raises her hands towards the car where Leonardo is sitting, as if blessing it and then letting destiny take over.

Amelia cleans up the house and herself just in time to hear the doorbell ring.

She opens it and is glad to see Amy. They hug each other and Amelia beckons her to come in.

Amy got herself comfortable on the couch, while Amelia gets coffee for them. Soon both of them were sitting and enjoying the hot beverage.

Amy breaks the silence, "Amelia I was thinking, how about we start our own knitting business?"

Amelia is skeptical since she does not know anything about running a business and with Albert not by her side; she does not want to risk their small amount of savings. Owning a business always has its ups and downs.

She looks down at her cup thinking of a way to decline Amy's offer gently.

Amy senses it and continues, "You don't have to invest any of your money. Just be my partner and knit. My husband already owns a plumbing business and wants to venture out in other directions. I suggested knitting and he agreed."

Amelia is still not comfortable.

Amy continues, "Our business will invest in wool and once we sell our knitting scarves, we will get divide the profit as 60-40. Is that doable?"

She waits patiently for Amelia to decide as she sips her coffee in silence while looking away to allow Amelia to think this through.
Amelia sips her coffee and thinks, "Sound like a doable plan. I don't have to leave the house and will be around Leonardo to listen to his new ventures and about his part time job at Albert's facility."

She looked up and placed her hand over Amy's shoulder, "Thank you Amy for this generous offer. I accept it. Tell me when can I begin?"

Amy immediately gets up and says, "I will be right back."

She goes out and fetches a bag, opens it to reveal catalogues and wool of different colors. She also takes out a few papers from her purse.

Placing everything on the table and scratches her head while announcing excitedly, "Where do I begin with?"

Amelia starts to laugh.

Amy gathers her thoughts and then picks up the various catalogues. She shows Amelia the various designs and patterns of scarves that people knit and asks her for tips.

They exchange views over many topics concerning the knitting and the patterns of the scarves and come to consensus quickly.

Both these ladies had an instant connection when they had met via the knitting club, and they respected each other's views and opinions and most of the time, agreed with it. This made them very compatible, so working together was never an issue for them.

Amy is aware of these compatible traits between her and Amelia and had thought of expanding their friendship into a business venture. Amelia is also comfortable with Amy and so, she agreed.

Once they share their to-do lists with each other and how to go about their first project, Amy picked up some papers from the table. She put them in Amelia's lap and declared, "Let us turn our friendship into a business partnership. I want you to read these terms and agreements of our business and sign here." She pointed towards a place, which had an X on it.

Amelia has leapt into this business venture, but however; she wanted to inform Leonardo before she signed anything. So she said "Amy I am pretty confident that Leonardo will appreciate my new venture, but I want to show these papers to him prior to doing anything official."

"Sure, Amelia, no rush. Take your time. Show him the papers and let me know when I can come by to collect them."
They shook hands and Amy departed.

Twenty One

Leonardo is having a hard time concentrating in his college. He keeps glancing at the watch every hour. Finally when all his classes are over for the day, he meets Sophia for a few minutes and that took the load of his anxiety for his next adventure of the day.

They part with a hug and a promise to speak to each other at the end of the day.

Leonardo sits in his dad's car and starts driving towards his facility. He has sweaty palms and wonders if he made the right decision to join his late father's place for work, but then realizes that his inner conscience felt comfortable and the path he chose was right. He nods to himself to tell himself that he is doing the right thing and parks the car in the garage. He steps out of the car, and says, "Let's do it." He starts to walk towards Mateo's office and does not even think of looking back.

He knocks on Mateo's cubicle and enters. It is a very small cubicle, which can accommodate only one chair. After their greetings, Leonardo sat down and looked anxiously at Mateo who is taking out some papers from his drawer.

After John Kemp was moved as a temporary warden, there have been changes in the guard department and the person to whom Mateo was reporting; Edward was made the head of the guard department. Mateo has also been promoted and the other guards reported to Mateo. So he is in charge of training Leonardo.

Mateo places the papers in front of Leonardo, tells him to study them and leaves him. Leonardo starts reading. Mateo returns after thirty minutes. Leonardo is still reading the papers.

Mateo asks Leonardo to accompany him for his walk into the grounds and gives him instructions. Since Leonardo does not have any formal training, he is expected to guard some low-key grounds. But he still requires some basic training before being handed a gun to protect people.

Mateo briefs him about the training, which would take a week after which he will be given a uniform and be expected to report for duty.

Leonardo listened attentively. He informs Mateo about his class agendas for the remaining semester so that his guard duty schedule can be arranged accordingly. Mateo offers to get his textbooks from the library since Maria works in one. Leonardo is grateful for the offer.

Leonardo reaches home around dinnertime and Amelia is anxiously waiting up for him while she is knitting.

When she hears the tires screech into the driveway; for a minute she thinks it is Albert since the car would make the same kind of noise when he would park. She drops her knitting abruptly on the couch, instead of placing it carefully in a bag.

Her heart is beating fast and she goes and opens the door. She sees Leonardo get out of the car and she closes her eyes. One part of her longs for her husband and the other part of her is happy that her son is back home safe and sound. She notices that he looks tired.

They both greet each other with a smile and a hug. Leonardo asked himself to be excused while he goes and freshens up. Amelia lays the table and heats the dinner.

Leonardo turns on the television and sits next to her for dinner. They both are conscious of the empty chair, which Albert used to sit on, but do not comment on it.

Amelia wants to hear about Leonardo's day and Leonardo eagerly tells her. About his weeklong training and then his regular duty. Amelia is not happy to hear about the training using the gun, but knows that a guard has to do his duty. So she just comments, "You be careful, son. You are dealing with criminals here."

Leonardo looks up from his plate and says, "Sure mom, there wouldn't be many incidents happening during my time of duty. I have only four hours of duty and Mateo stated that it will be in a safe location, comparatively."

Amelia inquires about the car. He shrugs his shoulder and replies, "What about it, mom? It is a decent car and in fact, I want to ride it everyday. It gives me fond memories of my time with dad."

Amelia asks him, "So what about your car that dad gifted you?"

He is hesitant initially but then says, "How about we sell it?"

Amelia gets a little irritated but realizes that he is making sense. So she says, "Okay. So how do we go about it?"

"Don't worry about that. I will post a few ads on my campus. It should be a piece of cake." He smiles with a wink.

"So, how was your day? Mom" he asks.

Amelia tells Leonardo about Amy and her new venture. She points to the papers, which were kept on the center table in the living room. Leonardo is excited and says, "Wow, mom you should go for it."

Amelia agrees and says, "The prospects looks bright and I don't need to invest much so, gave her a verbal yes, but thought of consulting you before I sign any papers."

Leonardo glances at the papers and agrees, "I will go through those papers mom, but you have known Amy for a long time and you both share good vibes so, I agree; your future looks good."

He smiles and puts a spoon full of rice in his mouth.

Mother and son are now together in this journey of life where they would encourage each other with their genuine opinions and hold each other's hand while getting past each day.

After dinner, Leonardo helps her clean up and then the duo sits on the couch, while Leonardo studies the papers. He seriously looks through each clause and tries to understand it. Amelia is proud of her son and the fact that he is taking interest in her life. It makes her emotional. She silently showers him with blessings as he is reading those papers.

Leonardo nods and gave thumbs up. He pulls out a pen from his shirt, places the papers on the table and gestures to his mom to sign them.

"Mom, let's close the deal. You are officially a business woman now." He smiles while saying the above.

Amelia gets teary eyes but smiles and signs the papers.

Leonardo presses her shoulder and asserts, "Mom you always keep saying that for a new beginning to happen, an event has to take place. Unfortunately, Dad was an event for this new beginning."

Mom nods, "Sure, Leonardo I agree. Unfortunately, this incident has changed both our lives."

Leonardo tries to look on the positive side and argues, "But mom, nothing is constant so, changes in our personal front should be faced like the changing of the season."

Amelia wipes her tears and brings her head towards his head and says, "You have become a big boy, my dear. Taking care of your mom and advising her, just like I used to do till yesterday." She pauses and then says, "I am proud of you."

Leonardo feels proud to hear these words.

When she finishes signing those papers, she keeps them on the side table next to Albert's picture frame. Then she shows him the various designs that she and Amy plan to work on.

They impressed Leonardo, "Mom, you plan on making such beautiful designs? I will be your first customer then."

Amelia chuckles with pride.

"No seriously mom, once you finish this muffler, I plan on advertising it in my school. Teens love this kind of design and in fact, I can even ask Sophia to help in marketing your stuff. She is pretty good at it."

Amelia is very excited with this new project and declares, "I will finish this as soon as possible so that revenue starts pouring in."

She picks up her knitting and with the television on; she starts working on it.

Leonardo is very happy to see his mom excited. He is thankful to Amy for coming and proposing this business venture. He gets up and goes to his room to finish some assignments, which were due the next day.

When he sits down at his desk, he gets a call. He answers without looking at the caller id, "Hi Sophia."

They talk for some time and he updates her about his first day at his job. Then he hangs up and starts studying while his mom is knitting outside with the television giving her company.

She knits for an hour, and then calls it a night. She wishes Leonardo good night and goes to bed. She has stopped resting during the day so that her thoughts would not wander at night. As soon as she lies down, she is off to wonderland.

She is thankful, since her heart still missed Albert especially when she sees the other side of the bed empty.

She has been meaning to clean up Albert's wardrobe, but has not yet been able to gather strength to open it and start sorting it out. Leonardo does not push her and thinks that when the time will come, it will be done.

Gradually the Silva household is trying to come to terms with the loss of the head of the family.

Leonardo is confident about his future since he is following the path shown by his dad and he knows it to be a secure one.

Amelia is trying to get a grip on her emotions by keeping herself busy with her knitting adventures, thanks to Amy.

Leonardo is too tired to study till late in the night, so he sleeps early, however; prior to tucking himself in bed, he peeps in his mom's room to check on her and then makes sure the doors were securely bolted. He is slowly developing a sense of responsibility and is confident that his shoulders would be able to carry the load.

A week passes by in no time. Leonardo's training is completed and he is issued a uniform to be worn from the next day onwards and was assigned to be a chaperone in the dining facility.

He went home proud of his achievement and showed his uniform to his mom. Amelia stared at it as if she was seeing the gray color for the first time. She then kissed the uniform and wished him luck with teary eyes.

Twenty Two

Convicts come in batches to the dining area to eat and then leave. Leonardo along with six other guards is on duty when the criminals eat to ensure that everything is normal. He is the only new guard in that batch and feels protected by other guards. The older guards ensure that he is not left alone with a group of criminals.

Leonardo gradually starts to get a grip on this job and gain confidence every day.

He is done with his last quarter in the community college and is getting emotional. This college is like his second home where he could come and shed a tear on any of its benches especially after his dad's demise and it would keep his secret. He managed to sell his car in this campus. His mom's business started soaring thanks to many orders from the teenagers who studied here. All his paperwork was transferred to his university. He informs his department in the university about his leave for a semester and resuming back after 6 months.

In those six months, he intends to give his heart and soul in his new job. He extends his hours of duty and learns new strategies to cope up with the captives and to communicate with them. John Kemp is still the warden, as the facility cannot find an appropriate head.

John keeps an eye on Leonardo's progress and is happy with it. He calls him every now and then and lauds his hard work. Leonardo's confidence soars after his weekly meetings with John. Sometimes, he wishes it was his dad doing that, and imagines how cool would have been if his dad was the warden and he was working part time under him. He grins thinking about all the special attention he would have got.

Amelia is busy with her knitting orders and she frequently visits Amy or vice versa to discuss the designs and strategies to meet the increasing demands.

Amy and her husband are happy to see how their baby just two months old was progressing and always thank Amelia for her contribution while giving her a fair share.

There are moments when the mother and son grieve over their loss especially when they share their success stories. They always start their conversation with, "What if dad was here, how would he react?" Or "If Albert knew that I have become a businesswoman, he would be so proud of me."

Fortunately, they have each other to ground them and keep them in touch with the realities of life, thus these successes never really turned their heads. They kept thinking of happiness to be temporary since sorrow always follows happiness and vice versa.

Since Leonardo had taken a break from his semester, his working hours are from 9am to 5pm at the facility. He wears his uniform and leaves for work daily. Initially Amelia avoided seeing him in his uniform but then as the days turned into weeks, she begins to feel comfortable seeing her son in it.

With seven hours on duty, he is given an hour off for lunch break and for his first three hours he is assigned to guard the kitchen when some convicts would come to cook, and the latter three hours to the dining area when convicts come to eat.

It is one of the usual days when Leonardo leaves for his duty. He parks his dad's car in the garage and reports for duty at Mateo's cubicle, where he collects his arms and goes to the kitchen. While walking, he feels some eyes are staring at his back and turns but finds no one. He is confused and thinks that maybe his mind is playing games.

He joins the other guards and starts guarding the kitchen while checking out the criminals who are washing dishes and cleaning the floors. He notices one person in particular, who is having problems in carrying out his normal chores and is limping. He observes him constantly then goes to check on him, "Is something bothering you? You seem to be doing your chores with difficulty?"

The person has a number 457 sewn on his prison uniform. Leonardo does not know his history or about his involvement in a case during his dad's time. The convict does not say anything, but just raises his trousers and shows the wound to the guard. Leonardo is shocked to see the deep wound and tells him that he needs medical attention. He pages one of the guards and asks him to come in. The convict does not speak but shakes his head as if denying any kind of help. Leonardo is determined to get his wound bandaged. When another guard approaches, Leonardo updates him about the convict's wound and asks for his help. They both are aiding convict no. 457 by his shoulders when he punches Leonardo on his chin. The punch is unexpected and Leonardo is taken aback. The other guard immediately drops the convict and pulls out his gun and points it at him. There is a lot of chaos in the kitchen as people stop working and stare at these three people.

Other guards hear all this chaos and come running from different parts of the kitchen towards them. One of them also paged for additional help. Leonardo stands there, shocked, holding his chin and trying to understand why this occurred. He has just tried to help the convict, so this reaction is unwarranted.
A guard escorts Leonardo outside to check his wounds, while a few other guards surround the person who hit him. He just lies there on the ground and allows the guards to hit him while they ask him questions. They want answers but he refuses to speak. One of them feels that maybe other jailers are intimidating him so; he suggests that he be taken to his cell for further questioning. They alert Mateo and pick up the convict and drag him to his cell.

Leonardo is also eager to get the answers so he reaches the cell where Mateo is questioning the convict, and watches from outside.

Finally after a few hours of torture, the man blurts out while crying loudly, "I was hurt by my cell mates. They were teasing me and I revolted and got beaten." He continues while wiping his tears and taking deep breaths, "I did not want to go and get medical help, since this would expose the incident and then my cell mates would hurt me more." He pauses and then persists, "I don't even know how much strength I have left within me to endure all this torture by my cell-mates who are mostly high and the visiting brother."

He was victimized earlier and since then his cellmates have picked him upon. There were many wounds inflicted on his body by his cellmates but he never had the courage to tell the guards and allowed his wounds to heal on their own.

Today he got caught and fears the consequences. Mateo is taken aback by the word brother, and is curious who this is and how is he affecting the lives of the inmates?

Mateo takes out the list of his cellmates. He asks the guards to summon them.

Just then he gets a call from home. His wife needs him home as their son; Pedro needed to go to the ER. He is a little taken aback, but can't leave this case hanging. Leonardo offers to carry on with the investigation. Mateo is a little apprehensive about handing this over to a new guard, but Leonardo's determination and his fiery eyes make him give the investigation to him. He assigns another guard to Leonardo and leaves.

Leonardo and the other guard wait for the cellmates to arrive. They lock the doors when the three cellmates enter and begin questioning them about the mischief and their various shenanigans. Fortunately for Leonardo, it was a quick session. The inmates are intoxicated and utter a name Carlos many times.

A quick research is done on who all visit these inmates in particular, and the logbook showed records of Carlos. Videos are pulled out of when this man in particular comes to meet and with close observation they saw something being slid into the pockets of the inmate.

The Sheriff alerts about a person with a dark skin, and a white beard, and Laurelwood is quick to make his move and arrest is made in no time.

These three convicts also have a track record of bullying new convicts, and their torture of this old man with severe wounds is not acceptable. These three men are punished for what they did by keeping them away from the rest of the community and in isolation for a couple of months.

Man is a social animal and he needs to mingle with others for his mental balance. Leonardo thinks that keeping them in isolation would make them reflect on their actions. That way when they are in the company of other humans, they will realize how important others are for their sanity and behavior.

Leonardo makes a report of the investigation and the action he has taken, kept it on Mateo's table and left for the day. The sheriff was moving expeditiously on this case because it took away his friend, Albert and the mystery of who was trying to ruin the reputation of that correction facility has been kept pending for long. He wants to solve this puzzle. His determination made him proud and weep as he was sitting down to write his report for John.

The next day when Leonardo arrives at the facility, Mateo and John felicitate him. They commend his judgment and appreciate his leadership skills. John shows the report of Sheriff Laurelwood where the pieces of the puzzle fit in perfectly giving proof of who killed the ex-warden.

Leonardo has mixed emotions and is teary eyed yet proud of his achievement. He could nail down the killer of his dad, made him feel heroic while also wishing for his dad to be around him at this moment to rejoice over his stouthearted achievement.

He took a couple of seconds to realize his thoughts and smirked at his analogy, while missing his dad at this juncture of time.

****

A few months pass by and the facility is still looking for a warden, since John does not want the position. Seeing Leonardo's progress, John is eyeing Leonardo for this position. He casually informs Leonardo about the warden exam coming up and makes him emotional with the memories of his dad. He also challenges him jokingly about taking the warden exam.

Leonardo is nostalgic after his meeting with John and takes up the challenge. He inquires about this exam and since he has a break from school, he studies for it by borrowing materials from the library. Amelia asks him about his intentions and he explains, "It is for fun's sake, mom. You know my goal of life is to be an engineer, John challenged me and I want to give this exam a shot since I am free."

Amelia goes with the flow and also challenges him with a wink and a hug.

In a month's time, Leonardo takes the exam and he clears it. He was very happy and goes to John with the results.

John is ecstatic and hugs him tight, "So, I am sure you would like to head this facility?"

Leonardo laughs and says, "Oh no, John. This test was just because you challenged me. I have my goal in my life and it is definitely not being a warden. I have seen my dad struggle and don't want to repeat history."

John argues with him, "But you cannot deny the pleasure he got by changing the lives of people who needed a new dimension. Every individual has a special purpose, and a special talent to give to others. He even kept a journal of it."

Leonardo agrees, "Sure, I don't deny that. He would boast of it for hours to come when he came home. I remember it. But the way he died still haunts me. The report that you gave me, still gives me goose bumps."

John admits, "I agree, his demise was a tragic one. But, many still remember him today. They have a high regard for his work," Leonardo put his head down and felt proud while murmuring something to himself.

John comes to the point, "So, what say? Would you like to put this name as your facility of choice? I am sure they will recommend you seeing your dad's name in your application."

Leonardo gets up and replies harshly, "No, John. I told you already, this is not my goal of life." He realizes his tone and apologized instantly.

John waves his hand at him and ends it saying, "Well, sleep on this thought Leonardo and we could talk tomorrow about it."

Leonardo just hisses at his comment, and walks back to his duty.

He keeps thinking about John's words all through the day. His inner conscious argues with him about his dream job and he comes back to the present moment. He keeps having such flashes throughout the day and is exhausted when he reaches home.

Amelia is concerned but he does not tell her, he blames his exhaustion on a stressful day. After dinner he retires early to bed although his mind is still wandering miles away. Morning takes its own sweet time to come since he hardly gets a good night's sleep. He holds his head in his palms and thinks to himself, "It will not harm if I get trained for the warden's job under John for another 2 months and then quit it saying that I did not like it. I can join back my college thereafter and John will not bother me and keep reminding me of dad and his works." He feels very happy with his decision and comes out and announces, "Mom, I am thinking of getting trained as a warden under John."

Amelia is taken aback by his decision. She stares at him asks softly, "So, what happened to your dream job? I thought you wanted that badly."

Leonardo explains, "Yes, mom, my intention to serve in the Silicon industry is still strong. I want to feel what dad felt as a warden and since I have another two months until I go back to school, I was thinking I get my self trained under John."

Amelia is confused, "Then what will happen after two months?"

Leonardo replies confidently, "I will tell John that I am not fit for this job and quit as a warden. I will join school thereafter."

"But is that possible?" asks his bewildered mom.

"Sure it is possible, mom. I am technically a warden, and can quit anytime."

Amelia is flustered yet amazed at his glibness and wishes him good luck.

Twenty Three

Leonardo reaches work and goes straight to John. John is expecting him so he calls him right in. He hugs Leonardo on hearing his decision to join. However, Leonardo does not tell him about his intentions of quitting after two months.

John calls up the Sheriff and starts working out on the paperwork so that he can be assigned this facility. Within a few hours John gets the confirmation and he calls Leonardo who is on guard duty and gives him the good news.

Leonardo and John shake hands, as a new journey is about to begin. Mateo is updated about his promotion, and is delighted and congratulates him. He whispers into Leonardo's ear, "I am confident that you will be a great warden. I see traits of your dad in you." Leonardo gets very emotional hearing those words.

Leonardo is humble while being congratulated by his co-guards.

He is supposed to report back tomorrow at John's office which would be his office after the training. Mateo puts together a quick send off party for him. His co-guards are very supportive and helped plan out the event for him.

Leonardo is filled with happiness and feels blessed to have such people around him.

The food is moderate but the warmth of his co-workers made his evening bright and radiant. That night when he reaches home, he cannot stop talking about all of them and how they treated him. Amelia listens attentively while thinking of those days when Albert used to express his pleasure to his family after coming back from work.

She feels blessed.

Leonardo's training starts and he enjoys each day. Every evening, when he comes back from work, he updates Sophia about his day and when home, he repeats all of it again for his mom. Days turn into weeks and into months and before he knows it, his training is getting near completion. He does not want his days to fly by so fast and wants to hold them, but unfortunately nothing remains still.

One fine Sunday morning he is in his room for extra long time and Amelia waits anxiously outside to have her breakfast with her son. She calls him for breakfast several times, but he just replies that he will be out soon. Finally, she knocks on his door and opens it. He is in the restroom with its door open, standing in front of the mirror and giving a speech. She is confused and asks, "What are you doing, son?"

Leonardo turns around, "Mom in one week's time I

will be an official warden of that facility and I am practicing ways to give my resignation speech to John." He scratches his head and continues, "Just can't find the exact words to say it, mom."

Amelia strokes his shoulder and says, "Come let's eat and then figure it out."

He follows her obediently to the dining table. They eat quietly. Leonardo is thinking about his conversation with John and Amelia is thinking of the best way to help out her son in this dilemma.

Then she starts, "So, tell me again, why do you want to resign?"

Leonardo is stunned by this question, "Mom, you know my passion is someplace else. I was just doing this because I wanted a feel of what Dad used to do and also because John challenged me."

"Sure, I understand. But, I hope you realize that only a few people get charged up with adrenaline when they are back from work and have great experiences of touching lives each day. You are blessed to be doing that."

Leonardo corrects her, "Well, not everyday mom. There were days when a particular person is resistant to change and has to be beaten up."

"Sure, but then eventually that person changes for the better, correct?"

Leonardo nods silently as he sips his coffee.

Amelia continues, "All of us are opinionated son, and when we are asked to change, we resist. So do these convicts in your facility. The programs run in the facility are so well planned out; thanks to your dad that if you continue being a warden, you just have to play along your dad's lines. It will be a piece of cake." She smiles.

Leonardo is a little furious and responds, "What do you mean? I am not smart enough to be on my own?"

Amelia is quick to respond, "I did not say that, son. All I said was that you like this job. It gives you so much excitement and joy on being able to change someone's life for the better. Maybe, you should stick to it."

Leonardo gets up from the table, "Excuse me mom."

Amelia keeps silent. She wants him to make his own decision.

Leonardo is lost. He is utterly confused. He goes to his room and dials Sophia and tells her about his dilemma and listened to her thoughts. He cannot sit for a long time as her opinion is the same as Amelia's. For a moment, he thinks both his mom and Sophia have consulted each other, but then he realizes that they will not team up against him and even if they would, it would be for his good. He abruptly hangs up with some excuse, but his mind is restless. Amelia senses this and suggests that he should go out for a walk.

He likes that idea, wears his sneakers and walks out, shutting the door after him. He leaves his cell phone at home so that he is not disturbed.

Amelia sits on the couch and starts knitting while her mind is with her son. She looks at her husband's picture and asks the holy spirits to guide his son in making the right decision, which will lead to his happiness and fulfillment in this lifetime.

She knits for an hour and then finally hears the door open. Leonardo enters looking very relaxed and comes and sits next to her. She keeps her knitting aside and looks at him anxiously. He puts his head on her lap and starts speaking, "Mom, I guess destiny has struck upon me as well. I am right now feeling so sad about leaving my goal in life way behind and letting fate take over my life."

Amelia strokes his hair and gets a little emotional hearing his words. She comments, "Son, unfortunately this is life. What we want from it, we seldom get. However, you should be happy that destiny has given you something that you get happiness from. Correct?"

Leonardo nods but continues, "Mom, I wanted that goal so badly in my life."

Amelia asks, "But why did you want that so badly in your life, son?"

Leonardo looks up with a frown, "What do you mean, why, mom. A computer professional is respected and he earns so much money."

"Son, even a warden is a reputable job. You forgot the praises your dad got from the mayor of our town. You forgot how he was given a send off when he passed away. A computer professional is just like any other human being and you will not be appreciated on such a level as your dad was acknowledged for all his services. Son, how much money do you need to live a life? A warden's job is sufficient to pay your bills and entertain you when you need it. Money is never sufficient if your desires are unlimited."

He listens intently and does not object. He nods but also laments, "But mom I am feeling so bad for not having seen that part of the world Maybe I would have aced it by becoming a CEO of a company. How will I know if I could do that?"

Amelia answers patiently, "Leonardo, the higher you go in any job, stress comes with it."

Leonardo says, "Mom, even dad was stressed out many times."

"Sure your dad would be stressed out at times. But his stress was related to an individual and his stubbornness while a CEO's stress would be related to some multi-billion dollar technology. The difference is huge, son."

Leonardo pouts like a school kid, "I agree with all the logistics, but I still wish I could see how I would fare as a techy. It would have been so cool."

He pauses and then continues, "I shall go ahead and change my plans of giving a termination letter with a solemn speech to John."

Amelia hugs him, "May be it is for the best, son."

Leonardo nods and gets up to ring Sophia and tell her about his plans.

Leonardo is not in the mood to do anything this Sunday. Amelia wants to go and get groceries and usually Leonardo accompanies her but, not today. He just sits on the couch and watches television.

Amelia leaves and on the way, she calls Sophia and informs her about his mood. She is quick to come and help cheer him up. When Amelia returns after her chores, she is happy to see Sophia's car parked near her home. When she enters, she hears Leonardo's loud laughter and is glad that he is not gloomy any more.

With Albert gone, she finds the quiet house unbearable. Leonardo was always there to either laugh or joke around with her or with someone on the phone. She is happy to hear the laughter and voices.

When he saw his mom arrive with the bags, Leonardo immediately gets up to help her and then announces that the three of them are going out for lunch. Amelia likes that. The three of them put away the groceries and freshen up to go out. Leonardo drives and Sophia sits next to him while Amelia is happy to be sitting behind.

The lunch is delicious and seeing the kids laugh fills Amelia with joy. However, she notices that Leonardo would slip away into a somber mood, but then would realize it and try to come out of it.

Realizing that Leonardo is still brooding about his change of career Amelia prays that night for Leonardo to get fulfillment in whatever he does and wants him to get a peak at his life if he would have been an engineer.

With that prayer in mind, she does not realize when she dozes off.

Twenty Four

Something magical happens that night. Leonardo goes on a ride and is able to remember all of it when the morning comes.

Morning dawns upon the Silva household. Mom wakes up and makes her usual coffee and starts cooking breakfast.

Leonardo wakes up, quickly showers and wears his jeans and a formal shirt. He is carrying a bag with a laptop in it.

Amelia and Leonardo greet each other and they sit down for breakfast. Amelia quietly reads the newspapers while Leonardo checks his emails on his phone. There is no conversation and food is eaten quietly.

Soon Leonardo gets up and bids his mother a bye and kisses her. Amelia says, "I hope to see you for dinner Leonardo."

Leonardo says, "I hope so, mom. I have a deadline to meet and I don't know how it will go. Will call you and let you know."

Amelia starts to clean up since she had to shower and get back to her knitting project.

Leonardo drives to work and after about forty-five minutes of commute, he parks in the parking lot of a company, titled, "HCL Technologies"

He gets out of his car and starts walking towards his building, with a laptop bag hanging on his shoulder and his phone on the other hand. He swipes his card to enter his building and nods at the receptionist as he walks by her towards the elevator, which will take him to the floor where his cubicle is located.

He goes into the elevator and pushes the button 4 and then starts to check his emails again. The elevator makes a ding noise as if to alert people to stop and look as their destination is here. Leonardo steps out and walks towards his cubicle. He meets many of his co-workers and they exchange greetings as they walk by each other. Then suddenly a man calls out, "Leonardo" Leonardo stops and looks back. He does not recognize the man so just waits for him to introduce himself.

"Hi, I am Zack" he extends his hand towards Leonardo and he adds, "I am a new hire and have been assigned to work under you."

"Ok so you are the new hire. I was told to mentor someone via email. I am glad to see you." Leonardo says with a smile and a handshake.

Zack asks him when he could come by for guidelines and assistance. Leonardo looks at his phone and says, "I have back to back meetings until 1pm. Why don't we meet for lunch and I can update you over that."

"Sure" replies Zack and goes his way while Leonardo updates his session in his meeting maker on the phone.

Leonardo goes to his cubicle, drops his laptop bag and carries his laptop and his phone to a meeting room. He greets everyone and they greet him back. Soon the manager comes in and starts to inquire about the bugs and is not happy with the status since the project's release date is close by. He requests his engineers to speed up their work so that success is achieved. Their success will be the success of the whole team. The meeting is adjourned, and Leonardo walks to another meeting room, where he meets engineering and discusses certain issues and they all try to brainstorm it. Time flies and it is 1pm.

He gets up to meet Zack for lunch. He briefs him about all the current projects and sends him an email while having lunch with him. He is working hard with not a minute to spare and does not look anywhere but at his computer screen, or his smart phone. Leonardo was already so tired since he can only think about his deadlines and racks his brain for solutions to them. Amidst all that, there is competition amongst the engineers. He is surrounded by negativity and stress of work. The sun sets and he is not even aware of it; since he is still juggling with his programming issues and debugging the product to be released.

The boss needs results, so he and a couple of engineers stay back and try to fix the problem. Dinner is on the house. Leonardo has been so engrossed in his work that he remembers his mom when he is taking his first bite of his burger. He calls his mom, who was waiting up for him for dinner. Since he did not call on time, she has made dinner for him as well. Now, she has to sit alone in front of the television and eat her dinner. She is unhappy; since such episodes are happening every now and then, but hopes that things will be normal once his team launches that product. Her son will be home on time.

After dinner, she continues to stay up for him, but then her eyes start to close, and she goes to bed. There have been days when she gets to see her son only in the morning, and that does not make her happy.

Leonardo comes home late. He sees the lights shut and creeps in slowly and goes to his room. He still has to reply to some emails, so he sits up in his bed with his phone and keeps doing that until his eyes force shut and his brain refuses to fight sleep.

In the morning he is up early and rushes again to work since he has an early meeting. Amelia has decided to go with the flow and does not bother him much with her constant questioning. She just reminds him to do some physical activity so that his body can take the stress.

He agrees with her and goes in to pack his gym bag to go for a workout before lunch.

While eating breakfast, Leonardo asks, "So, Mom how is your knitting business coming along? Have any new orders come lately?"

Amelia is very happy to hear that question and starts the story of her orders, but unfortunately she is interrupted by a phone call for Leonardo, which he has to take. He then leaves for work before Amelia could finish updating him about her work. She is taken aback, but then she realizes that it is his work that is pushing him to extreme levels, and that he had no intentions of hurting her feelings.

She forgives and forgets and starts her day with cleaning and showering and getting to work.

Leonardo's day goes by in troubleshooting and meetings. No one wants to take the blame of errors and they tend to lose their temper when fingers are pointed towards them for any glitch. The long hours of work with no rest wears out a person physically as well as emotionally, and it has led to such irrational attitude among all the co-workers.

Finally after weeks of late nights and the hard work by many workers, the product is being launched. There is a huge launch party in their office that evening and there is good food and champagne was flowing like water. Leonardo's boss is being appreciated for directing this project to success. The engineers were also thanked for all their hard work and a bonus check is given to all those who worked towards its success.

Leonardo is one of them. He looks at the check and kisses it. It was a huge one. As usual, he comes home late, but is quick to go to bed and he sleeps like a log.

Amelia wakes up the next morning and is very careful not to make any noise since she is aware of her son's product release last evening and she wants him to rest well. Leonardo sleeps till late and then when he wakes up, he is busy with his emails of congratulations. However, this time he is updating his mom about everything about the party and then he shows the check to her. Amelia is thrilled to see her son so happy after months and wishes him to stay in high spirits all the time.

That day at work, Leonardo is assigned another project and thus, the saga of reading and researching on the new project starts and he is gradually being sucked into the quicksand of stress and long working hours.

Amelia is getting tired of all this, and wishes that he gets a few more hours in a day to relax and have a personal life.

Sophia has finished school and has moved back to town. She has taken up a job as an elementary teacher in a school nearby and compared to Leonardo she has a flexible schedule is always waiting for Leonardo's call and hoping to meet him, but Leonardo can only meet on Friday evening and weekends, since on the other days Leonardo is mostly at work and comes home pretty late.

Sophia and Amelia are getting used to Leonardo's schedule and always treasure his company. Leonardo is aware of this and is grateful to them for understanding his hectic schedule.

Leonardo is growing technically but is always surrounded by stress, which is always compensated with a big check. This is gradually affecting his relationship with Sophia who is getting restless about their relationship status, but Leonardo is too ambitious to commit at this point and keeps delaying it.

So Sophia takes the other route. She starts ignoring his calls and always comes up with some excuse to avoid meeting him. Leonardo does not understand her behavior until one Saturday noon when he is relaxing in front of the television his mom explains it to him. He is upset but then realizes that it is high time he comes to a decision as well. So, he gets up, and goes to Sophia's house without calling her in advance.

Sophia's mom, Hua opens the door as she and her husband, Vincent are about to step out. She calls out to Sophia who was in her room and asks Leonardo to be seated, and they leave. Sophia is surprised to see Leonardo without any notice, but was still happy to see him. She wants to go and hug him, but keeps her distance and just says a plain, "Hi".

She sits opposite Leonardo, but Leonardo gets up and sat next to her. He pulls out something from his pocket and places it in her lap. It is an envelope. She frowns as she looks at it, glances at him and then opens it. It has a piece of paper in it. She opens it and starts to read. After she finishes reading it, she is ecstatic and hugs him while constantly saying, "Wow, I am so happy for you. Congratulations."

He corrects her, "You should be happy for us, my dear. It is your patience and my perseverance towards my job that I have been able to reap this result. I am thankful to you."

Sophia takes all those complements as her due since she knew it is not easy being quiet near a person who is always staring at his blackberry and using his fingers constantly on that phone while he is in company.

Sophia hugs him and then asked, "So, now what?"

Leonardo came down to her feet and said, "Now, we get engaged."

She beams with joy and her heart starts fluttering like a train and her face is red. She covers her mouth with both her hands, since she is drooling at the ring.

Then she realizes that Leonardo needs her left hand so she wipes her hand on her dress and extends it delicately towards him.

He places the ring on her finger and they exchange a kiss.

Sophia flutters like a bee from the couch and announces, "Oh, I got to announce to my parents, your mom, our friends. I have so much work to do."

Leonardo went back to his phone checking his emails, and said with a smile, "Sure, honey. Let's do it."

While Sophia is busy making phone calls to all, Leonardo is patiently sitting beside her and speaks to the friends and family when the phone would be passed on to him, otherwise; he is busy tapping his fingers on his blackberry.

Sophia does not mind Leonardo checking his emails. She is just glad that she could give a name to their relationship since peer pressure was eating her alive.

After hearing the good news, her parents came rushing in and hug Leonardo and Sophia. Hua is delirious hearing her daughter engaged that she calls up Leonardo's mom, "Hi Amelia. I am sure you heard the good news. So, let's celebrate. Please get ready and we will come by to pick you up." Hua is excited, and after hanging up, she announces that she needs to get ready. Sophia interrupts her, "Mom, you already look good. Remember, you just came from outside."

Hua turns to her daughter, "No, I have a special dress for this occasion. I have dreamt of this for a long time. I have to go and change."

The kids laugh and so does Vincent, Sophia's dad.

Hua takes a long time and Sophia has to go in to help her. Finally, Hua comes out looking younger than Sophia. She has lots of makeup on her face and her dress was shimmering. Leonardo has to force himself to say, "Wow"

Sophia winks at him.

Hua looks at Vincent as if wanting to hear something from his mouth. Vincent does not realize it until Sophia said it loud, "Dad, you ought to compliment mom."

"Do I have to?" Vincent asks innocently.

"Yes, you have to," orders Hua.

"Okay then, you look double wow," says Vincent in a flustered tone.

They all start to laugh. The parents decide on a venue and asked the children to meet them there. They go to pick up Amelia

Sophia and Leonardo reach the restaurant before them and are sitting on their designated table.

Sophia keeps flaunting her ring either to Leonardo or pretends to brush her hair while showing off that ring. Leonardo is grinning at all this. He confides something important to her. She first frowns and then nods with assurance.

Soon their parents arrive and are seated next to the couple. They all rejoice at a new beginning and Amelia is happy to see the blissful faces. Leonardo is watching his mom and is glad to see her cheerful on this special occasion.

Once lunch done, Sophia accompanies her parents while Leonardo leaves with his mom. Amelia is quiet when he was driving so he asks, "Are you happy, Mom?"

"Oh definitely son. I am just thinking of your dad. If he would have been around, he would have been jollier than Hua."

Leonardo objected, "No, Mom I am sure the way her mom was dressed for this occasion, no one could beat it. Not even dad would have."

They both start laughing.

Leonardo had asked Sophia about staying with Amelia after their marriage and Sophia agreed with some apprehensions. Amelia is aware of this mutual decision between them and is very happy. She wants them to get married soon so that she would not have to wait up for Leonardo alone anymore.

Soon a date is fixed and all preparations are done.

Amelia has no hang ups regarding the rituals of their wedding so she allows the Pham family to marry off their daughter in Vietnamese style. Leonardo is also okay dressing up according to their style. Amelia has called her parents from Portugal to be a part of her happiness. The day Leonardo is getting married is an emotional day for Amelia. She is recollecting her day of marriage and was imagining how Albert would have reacted on his son's wedding.

Once the honeymoon is over, Leonardo goes back to work after a week off and Sophia went back to her school. Amelia goes back to taking more orders for her knitting. Amy and she are thriving in this business.

As the days roll on, the long hours of work for Leonardo are back. He is getting compensated for his hard work by big bucks as a result they move into a bigger home and buy new cars. Albert's car is still sitting in the garage.

Luxuries are coming into the Silva household but the time to bond with each other is gone. Their bank balance stated big figures, but the happiness is invisible. There is bitterness between Sophia and Leonardo as a result they fight for petty reasons. Amelia initially tries to intervene but that worsens things. Thus, she just stayed in her room whenever she heard loud noises between them.

Leonardo is always stressed over deadlines and wants to ace all his projects. He is not good at taking failures so well especially since he knows he has it inside him to excel thus always wants to push for success.

Since his personal life is in shambles, it is making him an emotional wreck and this is affecting his health. It starts with some acute back pains for a few months, which he neglects due to time and is now chronic. The pain affects him while asleep or awake.

Twenty Five

This pain wakes him up. Human beings are unable to tolerate pain of any kind. Even though, all this is a dream, the pain jolts him awake He looks around the room and his bed, and takes a while to realize that all that was a dream and wipes his forehead and utters a loud "Phew"

He is relieved and starts reviewing his dream while pressing his back as if it is still hurting.

Amelia peeps in when she hears his loud Phew and seeing him pressing his back inquires, "What happened, Leonardo? Are you okay?"

Leonardo starts to blurt out his dream. She sits down next to him patiently listening to each detail, and thankful that he was able to see his future if he would have followed the goal of his life.

When narrating his dream, he mentions monetary gains many times, but then towards the end when he was getting emotional, and physically drained, he comments, "What help is this money, if it gives so much tension and stress to my life with you, and Sophia?"

Amelia is pleased to hear this and adds, "What will make you truly wealthy is the joy that you receive from giving your knowledge to others. That joy is only possible if you take up the job of a warden." She sees that his hand is still pressing his back and inquires if it pains. He becomes conscious of it and brings the hand forward since there is no pain anymore.

Amelia realizes that Leonardo needs some time to justify his inner conscious of destiny taking over his goal in life and try to make his peace with it. So she leaves him with the pretext of making breakfast.

Leonardo just sits there and starts realizing how hectic his life would be if he follows his dreams. For a moment, he goes back to his dream where he has bought that big house and how they renovated it with the latest gadgets. A smile also comes onto his face, when he reminiscences the new car he bought for himself, and how his mom and Sophia used to love going for a drive in it, but he also realized how little time he spent with them. He also felt pain in his heart to see how his mom used to be all-alone in the house when he worked overtime as a bachelor.

There are perks for working hard, and he sees those benefits in the form of a new home, car and so many luxuries in the house, but then when he recalls the fights and bitterness between him and Sophia and also the stress. He feels that he should open his fist and flush his dream into the toilet. He gets up to simulate this by going into his restroom, and when he pretends to throw his ambition into the toilet, he hesitates to flush and keeps staring at the toilet. He was attracted towards the money, the riches and luxuries, but then when he felt that excruciating pain in his back and in his heart over emotional and physical distress, he quickly flushes it and goes outside.

The material world that he longed for has taught him some important keys to happiness.

He is a whole new person when he sits for breakfast. He is content and happy. He intends to create his own world by changing his approach and choose to focus on ways to get joy and fulfillment by being aware of his actions.

Amelia sees those expressions on his face and is full of gratitude that her son has made his peace with destiny and is allowing fate to take over while controlling his own choices.

Made in the USA
Charleston, SC
29 October 2013